Totem Tales

LEGENDS FROM THE RAINFOREST

E. C. (Ted) Meyers

hancock
house

ISBN 0-88839-468-3
Copyright © 2005 E. C. (Ted) Meyers

Cataloguing in Publication Data

Meyers, Edward C.
 Totem tales : legends from the rainforest / E.C. (Ted) Meyers.

ISBN: 0-88839-468-3

 1. Indians of North America—Northwest, Pacific--Folklore.
2. Legends—Northwest, Pacific. I. Title.

E78.N77M482 2001   398.2'089'970795   C00-911514-5

Printed in South Korea — PACOM

Production: Mia Hancock

We acknowledge the financial support of the Government of Canada through the Book Publishing Industry Development Program (BPIDP) for our publishing activities.

Published simultaneously in Canada and the United States by

HANCOCK HOUSE PUBLISHERS LTD.
19313 Zero Avenue, Surrey, B.C. V3S 9R9
(604) 538-1114 Fax (604) 538-2262

HANCOCK HOUSE PUBLISHERS
1431 Harrison Avenue, Blaine, WA 98230-5005
(604) 538-1114 Fax (604) 538-2262
Web Site: www.hancockhouse.com *Email:* sales@hancockhouse.com

Contents

Raven Frees the People

A Haida Legend

One day, long ago, Loon was swimming about on a great ocean that covered the entire world. He was alone for in all the world there was no land for other living things. Loon was very lonely. He wished with all his heart that he might find some companionship. He had searched for many years, but the years had passed and he had found no one. Loon knew he was, except for the fish and whales who lived under the water, the only living creature in the world.

Suddenly, Loon looked up and saw a cloud in the sky. On the cloud was a great lodge of the type that had been so numerous before the water had come to flood the earth. Loon flew to the house and landed on the front porch.

As Loon looked into the open doorway, he spied a very old man sleeping in front of a fireplace in which burned a bright fire. The fireplace, Loon noticed, was made of a crystal-like material into which had been carved figures which he recognized as likenesses of the people who had inhabited the land before Great Spirit sent the flood. There was no one else in the house. The old man was alone.

Loon crept into the house. He stayed some time sitting before the fire warming his chilled body. He remained very quiet for he did not wish to awaken the old man. When he was warm enough, he returned to the porch where he began to shout out very loudly *Hulloah! Hulloah!* in greeting much as loons do to this day. The old one did not awaken. Loon called out many times but the old man remained sound asleep. Loon continued calling all through the rest of the day and into the night. Still, the old man remained asleep.

When evening fell at the end of the second day the ancient one awoke and came to the door.

"Loon," he asked, "why are you making all this noise?"

"I am lonely," replied Loon. "I crave company. I had hoped you would make me welcome."

"Ah," said the old one, "I understand. I take it you are lonely for the people who lived upon the land before the flood."

"Yes," Loon answered. "I pine for their company. Once there were many people and they were all my friends. Now they are gone, there is no land, the houses are all gone and I am alone. I feel much sorrow in my loneliness."

"It is time, then, to restore the earth to what it was before the flood," said the old man. "I will do that with your help."

The elderly wizard took a stick from a small box that had been standing in a corner of the room. He turned the stick over many times as he very carefully peeled away all the bark. Then he turned the stick very slowly through the smoke from the fire until it was just the right color. Slowly, he stroked the stick in great solemnity while he chanted magic words. The stick took the shape of a human boy. Then the wizard pulled slowly on the arms and legs until the boy had been stretched into the height of a full-grown man, perfect in every detail. But the wood still had no life within it.

The wizard then went into another room. When he came out again, he held a box. Inside the box was another and within it there was yet another, each one smaller than the other. There were five in all. From the fifth, the smallest box, the wizard took two black stones. One was small, the other a little larger. He handed the stones to Loon.

"Take these stones to the world below," he commanded. "Place the smallest one in the water and blow on it five times. You must be exact or the stone will sink and be lost forever."

"I understand, oh mighty wizard," said Loon, taking the stones.

"Then," continued the wizard, "you will drop the second stone into the water. This one you must blow upon as much as you can. You will grow tired but you must continue without letup until the setting of the sun. These stones will become the lands upon which the people will dwell."

Loon, very carefully, carried the stones to the world below. He faithfully carried out the wizard's instructions. As he blew on the stones, he noticed them becoming larger by the minute.

When he had completed the task, Loon flew high into the sky. As he glided on an air current he noticed the smaller stone had grown very large and had then divided into two islands. These islands Loon named Haida-Gwaii which means Hither Land. He watched as the large stone grew into a huge land which stretched in all directions farther than his eyes could see. This land Loon called Kwa'gaqui which means Yonder Land. Today the two islands are also called the Queen Charlotte Islands. The large land is called North America.

Loon then returned to the house in the sky to tell the wizard that he had completed the task. The old one looked down on the world and was pleased with what he saw. He sang a song of praise to Loon, which pleased Loon greatly as many years had passed since he had heard a song of praise sung on his behalf.

The wizard then breathed life into the figure of the human man which he had fashioned from the stick.

"Go to the earth with Loon," he told the man. "Loon will teach you all you will have to know in order to pass two tests. Loon will be your friend and companion as you learn."

Loon carried the man safely to the largest island. There they spent many years wandering about Haida-Gwaii while Loon taught the man all that he had to know.

Finally one day Loon said to the man: "You are now ready to attempt the two important tests which will restore the people to the earth. When the waters flooded the world, Great Spirit hid the spirits of the people in a clam shell so they would not be lost for all time. You will free them and become their leader. But, before you can become their leader you will have to find the clam shell in which they are hidden. That is the first great test. If you are successful, you will change into a raven.

"Then you will be ready for the second test, and that will be for you to coax the people to come out of the clam shell. They will not want to come out for they feel safe within it. You will have to use all the knowledge I have taught you to convince them to emerge. If you are successful in the second great test you will become a Supernatural Creature with great powers. You will then be known for all time as Raven-Who-Walks-The-Earth. You will teach the people all I have taught you."

Loon then said goodbye to his friend and left. He returned to the lodge in the sky. From there he and the wizard watched as the man set out on his tasks.

Though it took many months, the man did everything expected of him. He found the clam shell and used the skills Loon had taught him to pry it open. The moment the shell opened, the man turned into a raven. He then urged the people to come out though they were reluctant to emerge for they felt safe in the shell. After much time had passed some of the people were convinced that Raven spoke truthfully and they left the clam shell.

Raven then called upon all his skills and after more time had passed more people came out. Then more emerged until at last all the people had left the shell. They greeted the raven as their leader; and as they did, the raven grew very large as the wizard sent to him the great magic he would need to lead the people. He had become a Supernatural Creature just as Loon had said he would.

For many years Raven-Who-Walks-The-Earth led the people in their new homeland of Haida-Gwaii until at last he felt they had learned enough to go their own ways. Raven-Who-Walks-The-Earth then departed to live in the Misty Islands so the people could practice the skills they had learned.

The people revered Raven-Who-Walks-The-Earth and he became a great god to them. They sang his praises and carved his likeness in totem poles. To honor him they made statues and carved brooches from jade and other stones. The people of Haida-Gwaii have never forgotten the raven who returned them to their lands. Neither have they forgotten Loon who brought the Raven to the earth.

Great Spirit Creates the First Otter

(A Kwakiutl tale)

Many hundreds of years ago the Great Spirit was walking through the land to meet his brother W'allus. (The Kwakiutl people called the Great Spirit *Q'an'iquel'ukwha*, which means the Transformer, because he changed people into other forms as rewards or punishment.) Along the way the Transformer met a group of Indians who told him of a very bad man who was robbing villages and causing much suffering among his peaceful neighbors. The Indians said the man had been a maker of stone tools and had been a good man until he became lazy and refused to work. Then, the Indians said, the man had taken to stealing and causing trouble. The Transformer told the villagers he would deal with the problem and went on his way.

As he passed close to a large thicket of alder trees, he saw an evil-looking man lurking there. The man was holding a long spear and the Transformer realized that this was the person the villagers had told him about. Because the man was waving his spear in a menacing manner, the Transformer knew that news of his coming had preceded him. He walked very close to the man.

"Why do you lurk in the shadows?" he asked.

The man did not reply but backed further into the thicket still waving his spear.

"Come no closer," he shouted. "I will kill you."

"You do not have that power," the Transformer told him. "It is I who hold the power over you."

The Transformer knew this man was an evil person and he decided to change him into something else so he could cause no more trouble. He shouted a magic word which caused the man to stop because he could no longer move. *Q'an'iquel'ukwha* then sprinkled the man with magic dust and the man fell into a deep sleep.

When he awoke a few minutes later, he had become a small furry animal.

"What have you done to me?" the little animal squeaked.

"I changed you," the Transformer told him, "because you became an evil person. For too long you have been a danger to others. From here on you will be a harmless clown."

However, the Transformer felt the new creature looked too much like Beaver and he knew the industrious Beaver would not take kindly to being confused with an idle clown, even on rare occasions.

The Transformer picked up the spear and attached it to the animal's rear where it became a long, pointed tail.

"Now," said the god, "you can be on your way. In future you will be called River Otter. Because you were lazy in life you will spend your days in idle play and will swim in streams and rivers and will amuse others as you slide down the muddy banks. You will spend your life performing for the entertainment of those who pass by. In that way you will atone for your evil ways."

The next time you see a river otter watch how he breaks open clams using a rock. He does this because the Transformer left him with one human attribute—he could use a tool. He did this so everyone would know the original Otter had been a human who made tools from stone.

Raven Creates the First Beaver

(A Tsimshian Legend)

Once, in a valley in northern B.C., there lived a Tsimshian woman who was different from the other women in her village. She had brown hair instead of the more usual black and, because she thought this made her special, she had grown quite haughty.

One day she decided to go swimming but discovered her favorite pool had become shallow in the heat of summer. She thought about it for a while then built a dam of saplings and fallen trees in the stream. Soon the water had backed up to form a fine pool for her use.

The summer sun heated the water to such a warm degree the woman stayed in the water a very long time. As she swam back and forth in the water, a part of her dress slapped the water causing a loud noise. She liked the noise and stayed in a long time listening to it.

When the woman left the pool she forgot to remove the dam she had built so the pool got larger until it was a small lake. This pleased the woman because now she had a place to swim every day. All day she would swim back and forth in the warm water listening to her dress slapping on the water as she swam along.

It got so the woman spent all her days in the water. She neglected her work, which annoyed her husband. And the villagers were alarmed as well because the lake was growing larger by the week. They wanted her to take the dam apart but she refused and she would not tell where it was. Eventually, both her husband and the entire village were nagging at her.

One day she was swimming when her husband and the villagers came to the edge of the lake.

"Come out," they called. "Return to your duties and take apart the barrier you built. It is causing the lake to grow too big."

But she refused to come out. Instead she swam slowly back and forth slapping the water with the hem of her dress. She knew she was annoying everyone and she was pleased at their anger.

Ka'ah, the Raven God, was also watching. He, too, felt the lake was getting too large, but he wanted the woman to correct the problem on her own volition. He flew down to the edge of the water and called to her.

"Good woman," he called, "you should listen to your husband and the villagers. It is time for you to stop this foolish behavior."

But the woman with brown hair just laughed at Ka'ah. She swam away slapping the water with her dress.

Raven, a very powerful god, was not one to be laughed at. He cast a spell over the woman. Her brown hair turned to fur and began to grow all over her. Her dress turned into a flat tail. Soon she had turned into a strange animal.

"Because you obviously prefer the water to the land," Raven told/her, "you will remain in this lake forever. Because you have grown lazy, you will spend the time working on the dam you have built. You can come out of the lake only to gather wood for the dam that will also be your lodge."

"Oh! Ka'ah," she wailed, "forgive me. I did not realize it was you."

"It is too late for apologies," Raven replied. "The spell is cast and will not be undone. From this time forward your destiny is to keep the lake you have created at its present level. In order to do that you will have to continuously work on the dam you built from morning until night."

Thus, was the first beaver created. Later, the woman's husband, who had grown very lonely, called to Ka'ah.

"Oh mighty Raven," he cried, "please return my wife to me."

"No!" replied Ka'ah. "I do not undo spells. However, if you wish to join her I will turn you into such an animal as well. That way you both can live together."

The husband thought about the proposition.

"It would be better to be with her than to stay here by myself," he said at last. "I wish to be with my wife."

So Ka'ah cast a spell by sprinkling the husband with magic dust. The man changed into the same type of animal, only he was a little bigger in size. The wife was happy to see her husband and together they worked to keep the lake at the proper level. After awhile both agreed it was not a bad life because they were together. As the years passed they had many small beavers. When Ka'ah saw there were too many beavers in the lake he took most of them away and placed them in other lakes.

The beavers' job is to keep lakes at good levels. Sometimes they forget and allow the lake to rise too high and sometimes they allow it to get too low. Generally, however, they remember.

Some say the woman's lake was Babine Lake, others say it was Takla Lake. Both are very close to each other. Both have many beavers.

How the Rivers Were Formed

(Many variations)

In the very early days, long before the people had been placed on the earth, Tyee Sahale, the Great Spirit, put animals onto the world. These animals were supernatural. They spoke to each other, walked upright and were very much like humans. They carried bows and other weapons, but they used them only to ward off evil spirits that stalked the land doing mischief and other evil deeds.

Among these animals was a large family of extremely big, hairy creatures who walked in sizeable groups journeying back and forth from one end of the land to the other. They also walked upright and carried bows, but because these animals were so huge, their bows were extremely long in order to suit the size of their owners. Because the bows were so long, it was awkward for the animals to carry them in their hand. In order to keep them out of the way, they slung them over their shoulders.

As a result, one end of the bows dragged along the ground as the animals walked. As they dragged along the tips formed furrows in the ground. Because these huge animals walked back and forth over the same paths on their circuitous journey, eventually the furrows became trenches. After many centuries the trenches became deep chasms.

One day Greatest Beaver, who was responsible for the courses of rivers and the formation of lakes, saw the chasms the hairy animals had caused. He realized these chasms were ideal for rivers and he caused them to be filled with water from several of the lakes he had formed.

Soon, the chasms were filled with water and the rivers were created.

Great Spirit Creates the First Human

(A Nimpkish Legend)

Great Spirit looked down upon his world one day and saw fish and animals and birds and was pleased with his work. Yet he felt unfulfilled. Something was missing. He thought about the matter for a long time and finally decided he should change one of his creations into a superior animal. He had even chosen a name for his next creation. He had decided it would be called Human. Finally he came to a decision. He would do it.

Who among his creations, he wondered, should become a human? He thought about that for a long time. He wanted his human to possess strength, but not too much. This disqualified Grizzly Bear who was far too powerful to trust with the type of personality Great Spirit intended to give his new creation. Cougar likewise would not do as he was too smug and besides, he ate only meat. Great Spirit wanted the first man to dine on fruits as well as meat. Fox was too sly and Wolverine was too ferocious. He wanted him to make just decisions and he wanted him to treat others kindly. The first man must be tall and this meant birds and small animals would not do. One by one he checked off all his creatures and one by one he disqualified them all. At last only Halibut remained.

Great Spirit considered whether Halibut would do. Halibut had plenty of strength—but not as much as Bear. He grew to a good size with good length and weight. He was a creature of the sea, which meant the human would not dislike the water as did cougar. Halibut also had enough intelligence that he kept from being eaten by whales and sharks. Great Spirit decided Halibut would do nicely.

Great Spirit cast a spell over the sea and soon a halibut emerged from the water. He swam to the shore of a nearby island and splashed onto the beach. There he cast off his gray skin, his fins and his tail. Great Spirit sprinkled him with magic dust and the creature grew two arms and two legs and underwent many other changes. Then Halibut walked into the forest where Great Spirit caused him to fall asleep. While he was sleeping Great Spirit sprinkled more magic dust upon him. This magic gave him the intelligence to think, to talk and to learn new skills. When he awoke, he had become the first Nimpkish man.

Raven Punishes a Village

(A Tsimshian Legend)

Many years ago, deep in the Skeena Valley of northern B.C., there was a village called Temlahem. The village nestled at the foot of a high mountain. In this village lived many people, all of whom were very mean to animals. Even the children mistreated animals because they saw their elders do it and thought it was a normal way to act. Only one man in the entire village felt compassion toward animals. He tried to get his neighbors to change their ways but no one would listen. Indeed, the children taunted him as he went about his business.

One day, high on the mountain that overlooked the village, a baby mountain goat became separated from his mother. Confused, lonely and hungry the tiny goat wandered around alone until he eventually came to the foot of the mountain. When he saw the village, he felt he would be safe because there were so many children. He did not think the children would be mean.

The little mountain goat was wrong. When he entered the village, the children began throwing pebbles at him. Then they chased him through the village keeping him in a circle so he could not escape. The little mountain goat became very frightened and soon grew so tired he could run no more.

In the meantime the mother mountain goat had been searching for her baby. She, with the help of all the other goats, had searched all the trails but had not gone down the mountain because they did not think the little goat could have gone that far. They were high on the mountain when one of the goats looked down and saw the children tormenting the small goat. None of them knew what to do.

While the goats were looking down on the village trying to decide what to do the kindly man returned from fishing. He had a good amount of fish and was planning his supper as he walked to his lodge. Then, he saw the children chasing the little goat who, by this time, was so tired he could hardly walk. The children were beginning to pelt him with large stones. Many adults had joined the children and were shouting encouragement to the children. No one cared about the poor little goat.

The kindly man dashed into the crowd shoving adults aside and pushing children as he rushed to the poor little goat. He picked the tiny animal up and cradled him safely in his strong arms.

"You are all evil people," he shouted. "Do you not know this tiny animal is one of Great Spirit's favorite creatures?"

The crowd shouted insults at the kindly man. They had forgotten the ways of their fathers and had forgotten the lessons Ka'ah the Raven had taught them. But, they did not interfere with the man when he strode past them with the little goat in his arms. He took him into his lodge at the edge of the village and there he tended to the wounds caused by stones. The little goat bleated softly. He knew he was with a friend and felt safe at last.

Meanwhile, the adult mountain goats had begun to descend from the mountain intent on rescuing the little one. There were so many of them, and they were moving so quickly, the drumming of their hooves disturbed the Mountain Spirit who awoke with a great shudder. The sudden movement within the mountain caused a massive mud slide. Tons of mud slid down the slope heading directly for the village below.

Ka'ah the Raven had been watching the entire affair from a vantage point high above. He had seen the children and the adults tormenting the baby goat and had seen the kindly man rescue the little animal. He thought of ways he could punish the village.

Then, he saw the mud sliding down the mountain and knew the entire village would be smothered. He did not care about the sinful villagers, but he did not want anything to happen to either the baby goat or the kindly man. He quickly left his perch and flew directly to the village.

Ka'ah was a great god. He could do anything, so great was his power. Within a second he was over the village. The mighty raven cast a spell on the kindly man's house. As the mud swept into the village it parted as it neared the kindly man's lodge, rushed past and caused no damage to the lodge at all.

Ka'ah, however, did not spare the rest of the village. He allowed it to be covered by the mud. By the time the mountain goats reached the bottom of the mountain there was no one left alive in the village. The village lay buried beneath many feet of mud and rocks. Only the kindly man's lodge still stood. He emerged with the tiny goat and returned him to the mother.

The goats then returned to their mountain while the kindly man gathered his belongings and set out in search of a new village.

Ka'ah, sitting high in a tree, sang a sad song for his children who had forgotten that humans are supposed to treat animals with kindness and respect.

How the Screech Owl Was Created

(A Tlingit Legend)

There once lived in a Tlingit village a selfish woman. She did not subscribe to the Tlingit ways of sharing with others. This woman was so unkind and selfish that she would not even share with members of her own family. She had no friends but she did not care because, as she saw it, being alone meant she did not have to share.

One day her husband returned from the day's fishing with a large catch of herring. He told her to smoke them as they would fill a need over the winter. He also told her to give a basketful to his elderly mother. Then he went hunting.

The selfish woman decided to keep all the herring for her own family. She prepared the smoke racks and sorted all the fish into proper sizes. While she was working, her mother-in-law came to ask if her son had set aside any of the herring for her.

The selfish woman refused to give her any. She said her husband had not said anything about giving fish to anyone. The mother-in-law insisted her son had promised a share of the catch. The two women argued for a while until, finally, the old woman grabbed a basket full of herring and began to fill her own basket. As she reached into the selfish woman's basket, the selfish one threw hot coals from the fire on the old woman's hand.

The unfortunate woman let out a dreadful shriek of pain and rushed away to find water in which to soak her burned hand.

Great Spirit was passing by at that moment disguised as a wren. He heard the terrible shriek and stopped in his travels to look into the matter.

When he heard from the village shaman how the selfish woman had not only refused to give her mother-in-law the herring she had been promised but had tossed hot coals on her hand as well, Great Spirit was displeased. He cast a spell over the selfish woman and turned her into an owl. Then he gave her the same sound her mother-in-law had shrieked when the hot coals had burned her.

That is why screech owls, when they call out, sound as if they are being burned by hot coals.

Why Hummingbird Has a Red Throat

(A tale of the Coeur d'Alene people)

Long ago the Great Spirit made changes to his world. He decided that some birds would become hunters, some would catch fish and others would keep the smaller birds and animals from becoming too plentiful. The reasons for these changes were that fish, birds and animals were all friends and none had enemies. Soon the world was overpopulated with creatures of all types. As a result, there was a shortage of food and everyone suffered.

Great Spirit decreed that the eagles would fish, the hawks would hunt small animals that lived in the ground such as rabbits and mice and the falcons would prey upon birds. Then he sat back to view the results of his changes.

Not many months had passed before he realized he had made an error. He still felt his plan was sound, but he saw that the large birds were killing too many fish, animals and small birds. They were eating so much they were gaining weight, which caused them to look ungainly in flight. Some had taken to walking since they were too heavy to fly. Great Spirit grew displeased with what he saw.

"If this continues," he lamented to himself, "there will soon be too few fish, animals and birds and the large ones will grow too lazy to fly and will, in turn, all die."

However, he was unsure of how to rectify the situation. He knew he must be careful in whatever he did because if he changed things back to how they had been, powerful evil spirits would see it as a sign of self-doubt. This they would see as a weakness and they would become emboldened to rise up against the Great Spirit. He did not want to fight a major battle against the combined might of the evil spirits.

Great Spirit, therefore, decided to go down to the earth for a closer look at the situation. Perhaps, he thought, the solution would be clearer if he could see the problem at close hand. He journeyed from his home in the sky to the earth.

He stayed many days watching the hawks, eagles and falcons as they enjoyed their hunting. He noted that once a fish, small animal or bird was sighted it had no chance to escape. Still, he could not think of how to change the one-sided hunt.

As he sat lost in thought, he fixed his eyes on a tall tree many yards distant. He sat focused on the tree trying to harbor all his wisest thoughts on the problem at hand. Still, he could think of nothing worthwhile.

Suddenly, a small voice startled him.

"Good morning, Greatest of all Spirits," the voice trilled. "You seem to be lost in thought."

Great Spirit turned to see a very small hummingbird sitting on a branch. He had not seen the bird approach. Neither had he heard him.

"Good morning, Hummingbird," Great Spirit replied. "You startled me. How did you manage to creep up on me as you did?"

"I did not mean to approach unseen, Great Spirit," Hummingbird answered, "and in fact I was not silent. You were so occupied with your thoughts that you were looking intently ahead. As a result you were deprived of your sideways vision."

Great Spirit sat in silence for a moment. Then, he spoke.

"You are trying to tell me something of great importance, my small child," he said thoughtfully. "Pray tell me what is on your mind."

Hummingbird shifted to a position closer to Great Spirit. He spoke softly for he did not wish to be overheard by others. It would not do to have any evil spirits who might be lurking nearby know that the Great Spirit was asking advice.

"Great Spirit," Hummingbird began, "when you gave the large birds the ability to prey upon the smaller creatures you left them with all their normal senses. This means that they not only have size and speed but they also have keen eyesight. They see the small creatures long before they themselves are seen and are able to follow wherever the small ones go. Once they begin their attack, it is impossible to elude them."

Great Spirit thought about what Hummingbird had said and agreed he was right.

"You are quite right, of course, small one," he replied at last. "But I notice that you and your cousins are not bothered by the large birds. What defense have you developed?"

"We need no defense against the large ones," Hummingbird replied. "We are very small and we dart about in such unusual patterns that they cannot focus upon us. Also, we are drab in color and not easily seen. For the most part we are not large enough to make their effort in catching us worth their while."

"Perhaps," said the Great Spirit, "I should give all the small birds and animals the same agility as I have given the Hummingbirds. In that way they could also elude the larger birds."

"That would serve a purpose, Great Spirit," Hummingbird replied, "but then everyone would be darting about in strange directions. Animals and birds would dart into each other's paths and many injuries would result."

"That is so," Great Spirit agreed. "How then will I equalize the situation so my large birds will not starve and my small ones will be able to survive in larger numbers?"

"When I approached you," Hummingbird said, "you did not see me because you were staring straight ahead. When one is looking in a straight-ahead direction, he cannot see to either his left or his right."

"That is correct," replied Great Spirit, "but how will that solve my problem?"

"At the moment all fish, birds and animals have the ability to see from the corners of their eyes. This is because you placed their eyes wide enough apart that the angle of sight is quite wide. If you change the angle of the hunters' eyes so they can see only straight ahead they will be unable to follow their prey when the small ones dodge and veer away. They will then have to turn their heads completely in order to regain contact.

"If you leave the small ones their wide set eyes," Hummingbird continued, "they will retain the ability to see from the corners of their eyes without having to turn their heads. That way they will be able to sight the large birds more easily and escape will be made possible. The game of survival will be made fairer in all respects."

Great Spirit considered Hummingbird's words for some time. At last he spoke.

"How often I have noticed that the smallest of my creatures are so often the wisest. You, Hummingbird, are indeed one of those. I will do as you suggest. From this moment all birds who hunt, the eagles, falcons and hawks, will be able to see only in a narrow, straight-ahead direction. All birds, fish and animals who are hunted will be able to see on a wide angle."

That is why to this day hawks, eagles and falcons cannot see to their right or left without first turning their heads in the proper direction; and it is why small birds, fish and animals have eyes set more to the side of their heads.

Great Spirit was very pleased with the idea Hummingbird had given him and decided he should be granted an award. He called Hummingbird to him one day and asked him if he would like anything special.

"Great Spirit," Hummingbird replied, "I am truly happy. The flowers supply me with food, the Spring Wind Spirit does not blow away my tiny nest and Autumn Breeze Spirit warns me when I must fly south to avoid the ravages of North Wind who brings the winter cold. I need nothing."

Great Spirit, however, still wished to reward Hummingbird. He noticed that the bird's feathers were very drab with little color.

"I will give you a medal of rubies," Great Spirit said. "Ruby is the color of loyalty and is given only for the finest deeds. You and your descendants will wear the ruby medal forever as a sign that I am pleased with what you did for me."

Then Great Spirit sprinkled magic dust upon Hummingbird and dark red feathers formed on his throat. To this day when you see a humming-bird going about its business you can still see the splash of ruby feathers on its throat. That is why the hummingbird is known as the Ruby-throated Hummingbird.

Why Rabbits Hop

(Variances exist from Ontario to B.C.)

Wabasso, son of Greatest Rabbit, lived during the days before the Great Spirit placed humans on the earth. Although he was the eldest son of Greatest Rabbit, he had been given no duties to perform. This was because he did not possess the same qualities as his father and brothers. They were brave warriors and wise in all ways but Wabasso was timid and lacked courage. Because of these weaknesses, Greatest Rabbit could not trust him to carry out the work rabbits were expected to do during the early days of the world. So, while Greatest Rabbit and his other sons were away digging tunnels under the ground, Wabasso was left to walk around all day exploring the world in which he lived. He eagerly awaited the day when he would be allowed to join his father and brothers because he knew the work they did was important.

Great Spirit had given all his animal children work to do so his great plan for the world could go ahead and he could place his humans on the earth. Beavers built dams to form lakes and rivers, squirrels planted nuts which caused trees to grow and birds spread berry seeds here and there so bushes could spread around the world. Greatest Rabbit and his sons dug tunnels beneath the ground. By digging tunnels beneath the earth, the rabbits made it possible for Air Spirit to go below the surface and bring air to the roots of plants and trees. The work they did was very important and Wabasso hoped that one day his father would allow him to take part.

Like all rabbits of the time, Wabasso walked upright, could talk and could carry his belongings in his hands. He knew all the other animals as friends. There was no animosity between the animals in the early days of Great Spirit's world. Wabasso, however, was neither as smart nor as brave as his brothers. Often the smallest things frightened him and he was quick to run away instead of sitting quietly for a while to think the situation over. This trait annoyed Greatest Rabbit because Wabasso, as eldest son, would normally take his father's place as Greatest Rabbit when the day came for the elderly rabbit to make his journey to the Land of the Supernatural People. However, Greatest Rabbit could not be afraid and Wabasso was continuously reminded of this. But no amount of scolding could cause him to overcome his timidity. Great Spirit was also concerned because he had not planned for his children to be afraid of anything. Even the evil spirits who roamed the world were unable to make the animals afraid.

One morning as Wabasso walked along a path in the forest he looked up to see a woodpecker watching him from a high branch in a tall fir tree. He knew right away it was Great Spirit because he recognized the Great Spirit's usual disguise.

"How do you fare, little rabbit?" Great Spirit asked.

"I am well indeed," replied the rabbit. "I hope you will soon allow me to work with my brothers and my father."

The woodpecker said nothing for a moment. Then he flew down beside the rabbit.

"I cannot allow you to work with older animals until you overcome your fear of unknown things," he said. "It is not good that you are afraid of shadows and the rustle made by the Wind Spirit as he passes through the forest."

Wabasso became very defensive. He drew himself up to his full height of ten inches, looked Great Spirit directly in the eye and replied: "I am not afraid of such things. I have no fear of Wind Spirit and shadows do not bother me at all."

Great Spirit, however, was not deceived although he pretended to be.

"Very well," he said at last. "I will watch you for several days. If you are truly not afraid of such things, I will allow you to go to work with your brothers." Then he flew away into the depths of the forest.

The little rabbit was very pleased. He thought he had convinced Great Spirit that he was as brave as the next animal. He looked forward to joining his family in their work underground.

The Great Spirit had not been convinced. He knew the little rabbit was trying to fool him and he decided to put Wabasso to the test. He went on a journey to the lodge of the Sun Spirit and there he told Sun Spirit what he wanted him to do. Sun Spirit listened carefully and agreed to the request.

The following day Sun Spirit, as usual, shone down upon the land and bathed the entire forest in warm sunshine. Wabasso, when he emerged from his hole in the ground was pleased to see the day was so warm. He ventured out, took his walking stick and walked quickly toward a clearing where he intended to sunbathe.

Suddenly, Sun Spirit concentrated a particularly bright ray upon Wabasso. It was so bright it caused Wabasso to cast a long shadow ahead of him. It appeared so abruptly that Wabasso stopped in his tracks. The shadow frightened him and he turned and ran. However, no matter how fast he ran the terrible shadow followed him. He stopped and the shadow stopped. Then he ran again and the shadow followed. No matter what he did, he could not elude the fearsome shadow.

As Sun Spirit moved higher in the sky it was not long before he was directly above Wabasso. Now the shadow was directly beneath the rabbit. Wabasso, the timid rabbit, was very frightened. He tried to get away by hopping over the shadow. But, the shadow stayed with him and no matter which way he hopped he could not lose his tormentor.

Finally, in a voice that showed his fear, Wabasso called out to the Great Spirit for help. Within a few seconds the woodpecker appeared.

"You told me you had no fear of such things as shadows," the woodpecker said. "Yet here you are in total terror."

"Oh, Great Spirit," Wabasso wailed. "This terrible shadow is an evil spirit. No matter what I do I cannot escape him. Please order it to leave me alone."

Great Spirit was very saddened. He had hoped Wabasso would overcome his fears and stand tall and brave, a worthy successor to his father, the Greatest Rabbit. Alas, it was not to be.

"Wabasso," Great Spirit said, "the evil spirit you fear so greatly is nothing more than your own shadow. Had you sat down for a moment and thought about it your fears would have been overcome. That is the way to set aside things that seem frightening."

Great Spirit sat silently for a moment or two. He was not happy that the faith he had held for Wabasso had proven groundless.

"Wabasso, my child," Great Spirit said at last, "I cannot allow you to take your father's place as Greatest Rabbit. Because you have failed the test, there will be no more Greatest Rabbits after your father departs for the Land of the Supernatural People."

"You will continue to live out your life as an ordinary rabbit and will share the world with your brothers. You will marry and have children, but none will be Supernatural Animals."

Great Spirit remained silent for a further moment.

"As a reminder of your timidity, from this day forward you will no longer walk but will forever hop as if trying to escape your shadow. Your children and their children will do likewise for all time."

Great Spirit then sprinkled Wabasso with magic dust and flew away. After Great Spirit had gone Wabasso decided to leave also. He felt very sad that he had failed what he now knew to be a simple test. Why, he asked himself, had he not tried to solve his fear instead of running away from it?

It was then that he realized he could no longer walk upright. Now he hopped along on all fours as if trying to hop over his shadow. Great Spirit had also added an extra reminder. As Wabasso hopped along he also stopped every few seconds as if taking some time to contemplate what it was he was trying to escape. That is why rabbits hop instead of walk.

Why There Are So Many Mosquitos

(A Nicola Legend)

Thousands of years ago when the world was very new all of Tyee Sahale's creatures walked upright, could talk and were all about the same size. There were many animals in the world but only a few humans, all members of the Nicola people. The other animals, insects and birds lived in their own camps. Everyone lived happily together in what we now call the Okanagan Valley. Everyone could talk to each other and were good friends. The humans could talk to the four winds and to the children of the winds. Even Tyee Sahale, the great chief in the sky, would visit on occasion usually in the form of a small bird or animal.

One day a strange tribe appeared in the valley. They called themselves Mosquito People and they were not friendly. They lived on blood and would bite other people and animals in order to suck the blood from them. However, because they were the same size as everyone else, they were easy to see and to avoid. As a result, the Mosquito People caused little trouble aside from being annoying to others.

One day one of the Mosquito People killed the small daughter of a Nicola woman when the girl was picking berries in the woods. The woman told North Wind what had happened. North Wind told the woman

31

that he would punish the chief of the Mosquito People if she could lure the chief to the lake.

The woman thought and thought until she had devised a plan. She climbed into a tree that overhung a deep pool at the lake's edge. Then she positioned herself so her reflection was visible in the water. When she was ready she called to North Wind who hid in a nearby bush.

The woman began shouting insulting words about the Mosquito chief, calling him such things as "long nose" and "whining voice." He heard her and came running to inflict punishment. When he got to the edge of the lake, he could see only the woman's reflection in the water. He jumped in thinking he could catch the woman.

As the chief emerged from the lake, dripping wet from head to toe and wondering where the woman had gone, North Wind leapt out from the bush. He blew a cold breath on the Mosquito chief who immediately froze solid. North Wind called to the woman who came down from the safety of the tree.

"The Mosquito chief is frozen sold," North Wind told her. "Leave him there and he will remain frozen until my brother South Wind happens by. South Wind will melt him into a pool of water and he will disappear forever. When his people see what has happened to their chief they will go away because this valley will become taboo to them. The valley will be free of them for all time."

The woman thanked North Wind who turned to leave. As an afterthought he reminded the woman that under no conditions should she do anything except wait until South Wind came by. She promised she would comply.

North Wind was no sooner gone, however, when the woman decided she would destroy the Mosquito chief herself. She lit a large fire, threw the frozen Mosquito chief into it and watched him burn. Before long, the Mosquito chief had been reduced to a pile of ashes.

Suddenly, the ashes were scattered by a playful baby wind who had not been in on the plot. Because the woman had disobeyed North Wind, the ashes were restored to life as they rose into the air. They all became tiny replicas of the Mosquito chief. The cloud of tiny mosquitos flew away toward a swamp.

To this day mosquitos are small and pesky. They swarm as they do because that was the way in which the ashes rose after the zephyr had blown them into the air.

Because they fear North Wind, you will never see mosquitos in winter, and because of the fire set by the woman thousands of years ago, they do not like hot places, fire or smoke. That is why you never see them in deserts or other hot spots. They can be kept away by lighting a smoky fire at your campsite. Mosquitos prefer swamps and damp forests because those places are usually cool.

Why the Okanagan Valley Is So Dry

(A Nicola Legend)

Centuries ago when the world was young and the humans who had just been created by Tyee Sahale, the greatest of all the spirits, still numbered in the dozens, an argument began between the Mountain Spirit and the Rain Spirit. To that time all the land had been equally blessed with rain and every year each area received the same amount as its neighbor. As a result all the land was covered with flowers, trees and bushes. Green grass was abundant. All that changed when the two spirits began to argue one day about which of them was the most powerful.

The Mountain Spirit claimed he had the greatest magic because his mountains were made of solid rock. "Nothing," he proclaimed, "can ever wear my mountains down."

The Rain Spirit, who was equally as vain, disagreed. "You are wrong," he replied. "My rain over time can reduce your mountains to hills drop by drop."

Tyee Sahale listened to the two foolish spirits with sadness but did not interfere for that was not his way. Instead he let them argue, hoping they would tire of the foolishness and make peace with each other.

As time passed, the argument continued until the Mountain Spirit grew impatient. He decided to prove once and for all that he held the greatest magic. He called on all of his great powers and raised a great chain of high mountains along the western coast of B.C. and Washington. These mountains, which we call the Coastal Range, rose so high that the Rain Spirit was unable to get his clouds past them. The Rain Spirit, enraged, called every cloud together and threw them all against the mountains. His idea was to wear down the mountains with torrents of water.

For a long time the rain beat against the mountains but could make no headway. The mountains remained as high as ever. As a result of the quarrel, the west side of the mountain range received so much rain that huge green forests grew and lush gardens of shrubs and small plants flourished. This pleased the Mountain Spirit because the trees made his mountains even more attractive. His obvious pleasure further enraged the Rain Spirit who threw more clouds against the rugged mountains. The battle raged on without letup for centuries.

Tyee Sahale was not at all pleased. Neither were the poor humans on the east side of the mountains who depended on rain to grow the plants and herbs they needed to eat and to keep healthy. The animals also suffered for they could not obtain enough green grass to eat. Most of the animals moved westward into the valleys between the western mountains. This in turn deprived the humans of the animals they depended on for food and clothing. The lack of rain caused the Okanagan Valley to become like a desert.

Neither Tyee Sahale nor the humans had any wish to see the valley turn into a great expanse of sand, so when the humans called to the Great Spirit for help he called the two spirits to meet with him in council. He asked them to cease their foolish quarrel.

"You are destroying my beautiful valley," he said. "My humans and my animals are suffering as a result of your childish behavior."

The two spirits looked down and saw the Great Spirit was right. Still, because it would mean having to apologize, neither wanted to stop the quarrel. Finally they agreed to a sort of peace plan. The Mountain Spirit agreed to reduce some of his mountain peaks sufficiently to allow a number of clouds to pass through so the Rain Spirit could sprinkle the land with enough water and snow each year to keep grass, plants and trees from dying.

"The rain," the Mountain Spirit insisted, "must never exceed a depth that would reach above a human's knees." He was afraid that he would wear weak if he let in too many clouds. He did not want the Rain Spirit to appear as the winner in the quarrel.

Tyee Sahale agreed but insisted that the water be distributed throughout the year and never all at once.

"What about the lakes?" the Rain Spirit asked. "They must remain deep enough for the fish to flourish."

The Rain Spirit, realizing the Mountain Spirit was getting the best of the agreement, proposed that enough clouds should pass through so he might also keep the lakes and rivers supplied with water so the fish could flourish. The Mountain Spirit agreed to that and the council disbanded.

"Very well," the Mountain Spirit replied. "I will allow enough clouds to get past my mountains so the streams and rivers that feed the lakes will be able to keep the lakes filled to a great depth."

The Great Spirit was not happy with the terms the two had agreed upon but decided they would have to do. Then the council disbanded

To this day the Okanagan Valley never receives more than about ten inches of rain and snow in a year while the west side of the Coastal Range receives a great amount. That is also why the grass on the Okanagan hills is brown most of the year and the trees are not tall. The small measure of rain supplied by the Rain Spirit is only enough to keep wild shrubs, flowers and trees alive as the Mountain Spirit and the Rain Spirit continue in their timeless battle.

As time passed, new humans moved into the valley. They began to cultivate fruit trees and soon large orchards were growing. However, because of the shortage of natural rain water, the people were forced to turn to irrigation devices for the water needed for their vast orchards. They brought water from the creeks high in the hills and from the lakes and smaller streams through large wooden troughs. In these modern times, pumps and sprinklers are used to water their trees.

This method of obtaining water will probably continue for all time for it is unlikely the Rain Spirit and the Mountain Spirit will ever resolve their foolish quarrel.

Why Humans Are Not All Alike

(A Siwash Story)

Tyee Sahale, the Great Spirit, decided to place humans on his earth. He called together all the Supernatural Animals and told them of his plan. Some were in support while others were against it but finally they all agreed that the idea was favorable. They formed groups to discuss what the new people should look like and after much discussion they decided that the humans should be distinctly different from the animals.

Tyee Sahale then formed two human shapes from a piece of clay. One shape was of a man, the other of a woman. All agreed they should be that of mankind. He then breathed life into the shapes and they rose from the ground and looked around.

"Something seems wrong," said the Great Spirit. "What is wrong with my creations?"

Discussion followed and it was decided that the humans had no color. They were too white, too pale.

"Yes, that is what is wrong," replied Tyee Sahale. "They are too pale. However, they are here so I will allow them to remain. However, I do not find them all that pleasing so I will send them to live in the vast lands across the eastern ocean."

That was how the first white people were created and why they started out in what we now call Europe.

Then Tyee Sahale formed two more human shapes from clay. This time he decided to keep them in the sun until some color had entered them. After a few days in the sun he breathed life into them. Once again he was displeased with the result.

"My humans are a darker color," he lamented, "but they are still not exactly what I had in mind."

However, because they were otherwise perfect in every way he allowed them to stay on his earth. This time he sent them to live in the vast lands across the western ocean. These were the first Asians.

He decided to try once more. This time he thought he would bake the clay figures in an oven. However, he left them in too long and when he removed them from the coals the figures were black. Tyee Sahale decided to allow them to stay also and he sent them to live in the great continent we now know as Africa. Thus, were the first black people created.

Finally, he decided to bake one more pair of figures. This time he watched very closely and when he removed them from the coals the two were perfect in every way. They were exactly the correct shade of brown. Tyee Sahale was extremely pleased. He breathed life into the pair and kept them in the part of his world he considered his favorite place. He gave them everything they needed, taught them all they had to know about their world and looked over their well being for thousands of years.

These perfect people were, of course, the first Indians of North America.

How Crow and Halibut Tricked the Oolichan Chief

(A Cowichan Tale)

In the earliest days of this earth all of Great Spirit's creatures lived together in peace and harmony. The tribes were made up of animals, birds and humans, and all lived peacefully together. It had been this way for many years. Each tribe elected its chief and sometimes the chief might be a bird, animal or even a man. Usually the smartest one of the tribe was the chief.

Living along the shores of Nanoose Bay was a tribe that had chosen as its leader a mighty crow. He was very smart and had great magic. He led the tribe for many years and the people were happy.

Every spring the oolichan, tiny fish that live in the sea, had come to Nanoose Bay on their way to more northerly waters. In an agreement struck years before by Great Spirit, Oolichan Chief and Crow, it had been agreed that each spring the people of Crow's tribe could net enough of the tiny fish to keep their lodges supplied with the oil needed for cooking and lamp fuel as well as other things. They only caught what they needed and nothing was ever wasted. So abundant were the oolichan that they never noticed the annual temporary decreases in their numbers. As part of the bargain, Crow promised to keep other fish from entering the bay during the time the oolichan were using it.

Then one year a new chief was elected by the oolichan people. He learned of the treaty that had been struck between Great Spirit, Crow and the former chief. He resented that a number of his people were being netted while they were feeding in Nanoose Bay. He became angry because he wanted to be known as the greatest chief the oolichan had ever known and did not want to see his followers depleted every spring. He thought about this and decided that Crow must stop the fishing. He became determined to do something about it.

The following spring, Oolichan Chief forbade his people to enter Nanoose Bay. He told them to feed along the shores but not to go in. They did not understand but obediently did as they were told.

Crow's people, waiting inside the bay, could not understand why the oolichan were not coming in. Their nets were ready but there was nothing to catch. Crow was also perturbed and flew out to a large rock and perched on it.

"Hallo, oh Oolichan Chief," he called. "Why are your people not entering the bay?"

Oolichan Chief rose to the surface and swam over to the rock.

"I have commanded them not to," he replied. "I object that your people are taking too many of my people."

"That is not so," Crow answered. "We take only what we need for the coming year. Nothing is wasted."

"My time is being wasted," the Oolichan Chief countered. "My people will not enter the bay."

Crow was angry and told Oolichan Chief of the arrangement that had been made years before with the agreement of Great Spirit.

"Then was then," Oolichan Chief answered, "and long before my time. How am I to know there was ever such an arrangement?"

"You can ask Great Spirit," Crow replied. "You shall have to abide by his answer."

But Oolichan Chief refused and swam away. Crow, angry but helpless, watched in frustration. Then, realizing there would be no further discussion, he flew back to his village to consider his next move. He knew he must do something quickly because, even if he could arrange a meeting with Great Spirit, so much time would pass that the oolichan would be gone. He walked slowly up and down the beach lost in deep thought.

"Hulloah," a voice called. "Why is the mighty Crow so deep in meditation?"

Crow turned to where the voice was calling. He saw it was his friend, the Halibut Chief. They had been friends many years and had helped each other from time to time. Crow perched on a log and told Halibut Chief the troubles he was having with the new Oolichan Chief.

"Perhaps I can help," Halibut said. "The Oolichan Chief is stubborn but he has very little intelligence. He is greedy and does not like anyone else to get what he cannot have. Come closer and listen well. I have a plan that might work."

When Crow had settled close to Halibut the great flat fish spoke.

"Tonight, after darkness falls, I and a great many of my family will swim into the bay. We will go to the far end and wait for your signal. You will go to Oolichan Chief and tell him that he cannot come into the bay because another great family arrived during the night. You will tell him that you will net them instead. Because he is not smart, he will assume you are referring to a second family of oolichans. Tell Oolichan Chief that you do not want his family in the bay because the other family will fight them off and your nets will be wrecked.. If that happens, you will tell him, your people will be unable to catch any of the second family."

"That sounds good," mused Crow, "but how will I convince him that the bay is full of oolichan?"

"When you give a signal I and my many brothers will all splash around in a great to-do. Oolichan Chief will see what he thinks are thousands of oolichans. He will be so envious that he will order his family into the bay. Then you can net the numbers you need.

"Just be sure he does not get any closer than the mouth of the bay. If he sees we are halibut even he will know he is being tricked."

The next morning, just as the sun was beginning to rise, Crow flew to the big rock and called out for Oolichan Chief. The chief impatiently rose to the surface.

"What do you want now, Crow?" he asked.

"I just want to tell you that you and your family cannot enter the bay. Another great family came in during the night and they will fill our nets. There will be no need to bother Great Spirit now. Please see to it that none of your people enter the bay."

Crow turned as if to fly away, but Oolichan Chief stopped him.

"Where did this other family come from?" he demanded to know. "They have no right to be in my bay."

"Perhaps not," Crow replied, with a dismissive wave of his right wing, "but they are there. I care little about who fills our nets. One fish is as good as the other."

"Wait," the Oolichan Chief called again. "You must show me this great family."

"Very well," Crow replied. "Follow me."

He led Oolichan Chief to the mouth of the bay and pointed toward the far end of the bay. His pointing was the signal to Halibut.

When Halibut saw Crow's signal he called out to his brothers who all began to splash about. They caused the waters to roil and boil. Oolichan Chief gasped in amazement. Then he turned and swam rapidly away.

"Good," said Crow to himself. "He has gone to gather his family to chase the intruders from the bay."

Crow flew quickly to his village.

"Quickly," he ordered. "Go at once to the shores and man the nets. Make certain they are positioned properly. Oolichan Chief will be leading his great family into the bay any minute now."

As Crow predicted, the great family of oolichan entered the bay in their thousands intent on chasing the interlopers from "their" bay. When they reached the far end, however, they saw only halibut feeding quietly on the bottom.

The Oolichan Chief realized he had been tricked. He shouted to his family to flee but it was too late. Crow's nets were already closing.

"Oh Crow!" Oolichan Chief called out. "You lied to me. Lying is forbidden. I will complain to Great Spirit about this."

"I did not lie to you, Oolichan Chief," Crow replied. "I told you a huge family had entered the bay during the night. I had no obligation to tell you that it was a halibut family. It was because you are greedy that you thought it was another group of oolichan taking over your bay. You could not bear to accept such a thing and jumped to conclusions. You were tricked by your own selfishness and greed."

In a calm corner of the bay the Halibut Chief turned to his youngest children who were swimming near him.

"Learn from this," he said, quietly. "Only one who is greedy or selfish can be fooled in such a manner."

Why There Are Two Figures on the Moon

(A Legend of the Frog Spirit)

When the moon is full and you look up at it as it travels through the darkness of the night sky you can see strange shapes on its surface. To some it appears to be a face, but to others it appears to be quite different. To some Pacific Coast tribes it shows Kwa'te, the Great Spirit, and his wife in their unending journey through time.

Of all his humans, Kwa'te loves those of the Frog people the best. That he loves them over all others is well known—but while some believe it was because the Frog People had done great service for him at one time or another, the Frog People know the real reason is because a beautiful princess had rescued him from the clutches of the evil Swamp Spirit. Because the princess, the daughter of a great chief, did this heroic deed, the people became known as the Frog People. They became very wealthy, were successful in trade and owned many blankets of dog hair or other rich vestments.

When the earth was very young Great Spirit visited often. He came to earth to confer with his Supernatural Animals, the good spirits and the shamans who led the humans. During these visits he heard complaints, made decisions and changed things that he deemed worthy of change. It

43

is because he made changes that the people called him Kwa'te which means "The Changer."

One day, according to the age-old story, while the Great Spirit was on one of his visits he decided to take the form of a frog. He did this because he was in a particularly swampy area and as a frog he could make better time by using the water instead of the pathways. As he swam along, he became lost in thought and did not notice that he had entered a part of the swamp reserved for an evil one called Swamp Spirit. Lost as he was in his thoughts, he continued on until he was deep inside the evil spirit's lands. The farther he progressed, the weaker his own powers became until, finally, he realized he had grown quite weak. He climbed up on a fallen log to rest.

As Great Spirit rested he took a good look around. It was then he knew he had ventured into a forbidden land. Even Great Spirit was forbidden to trespass into areas that had been, by agreement, reserved for the evil ones. He began to worry about how he would get out without being discovered.

Alas, it was too late. Swamp Spirit had already spied him and appeared before him disguised as a water snake.

"You are my prisoner, Great Spirit," the evil one called out, "and by the agreed laws you are required to grant my wish."

"I am fully aware of the laws, evil one," Great Spirit replied, "and I do not need you to remind me of what I must do. As you are also aware of the laws, you know that because you are a spirit of the night your powers are very weak by day."

"At this moment, Kwa'te," the evil one answered, "my powers are neither greater nor lesser than yours. However, you are correct. I cannot force you to accede to my wishes until darkness falls. So, if you think you can escape from my swamp before nightfall you had better get busy. There is little left of the daylight."

Great Spirit knew the swamp spirit had the upper hand but he also knew he had some magic left. He decided he must use it quickly if he was to thwart the evil one. If he failed, he knew the evil spirit would force him to grant some concession.

"If I fall under your power, evil one," Great Spirit called out, "what will you ask of me?"

"I will demand that you grant me the power to dominate the tides of the oceans and the courses of rivers so that I might gain jurisdiction over all the earth's water. Brackish swamps are not a suitable kingdom for one of my great talents, so I want to control fresh water as well. With such control I will rule over the fish and through them I will gain dominion over the humans who depend on fish for food. With such power I will become the dominant spirit, more powerful even than you. That is what I will require."

"I will not grant you such a wish, evil one," replied great Spirit. "I will never agree to such a concession."

"In that case, Great Spirit, you will become my prisoner for all time. Without you to guide the world along its course, chaos will reign. The good spirits will be forced to struggle against the evil spirits for control. They will manage only to destroy each other and I will then emerge dominant because I will not enter the fray. I will become the greatest spirit and then I will take your place."

Great Spirit knew Swamp Spirit was right in what he said. The lesser spirits of good and evil would indeed destroy each other in a long battle for supremacy. It would be the animals and humans who would become the greatest losers. Great Spirit knew Swamp Spirit would be the most dreadful spirit ever to rule. He knew he would have to do something to escape from the swamp. Unfortunately, he had no idea of what he could do.

At first he tried to call out to Sun Spirit in hopes of having him halt his journey across the sky. If he could manage to stop Sun Spirit, he would have a continuous day and with it time to work out a suitable plan. However, no matter how loudly he called, he had grown too weak to cast his voice across such a distance. He sat back to think of something else.

Then, he decided to swim out of the swamp the same way he had entered. He leapt from the log and began to swim but, before he had gone more than a few feet, he realized he had become so weak he would not be able to continue. Weak of limb and heavy of heart, he climbed back onto his log. He feared the Swamp Spirit had bested him.

It was then that he saw a canoe approaching. The canoe was being paddled by a young woman who had been harvesting medicinal herbs and roots deep within the swamp. She was hurrying in order to be clear of the swamp before night fell. She was well aware of the evils that befell people who were caught at night in the swamp.

Great Spirit knew the woman was his last hope of escaping Swamp Spirit. He called out to her.

"Hello, good woman. Steer your canoe close that I might talk to you."

The young woman, fearful that the voice was that of an evil spirit, increased her paddle stroke. The canoe began to gain speed. Great Spirit, realizing that she was not going to heed his call, used most of his last ounces of magic to force the canoe to stop and move toward him until it touched against the log upon which he sat.

As the canoe came to rest against the log the woman recoiled in terror. She was afraid of swamp creatures and did not like frogs at all. She wanted only to avoid this one. Because it talked to her, she knew it was a spirit—probably an evil one because it was in the swamp.

"Do not be afraid," the frog said. "I am not an evil spirit. I am a good spirit being held prisoner by Swamp Spirit. I must escape before darkness or a great calamity will befall the earth and all the people."

The woman was not convinced. Instead of answering she tried to turn her canoe away from the log. Great Spirit's magic was almost used up but he managed to keep hold of the canoe.

"I am not an evil spirit," the frog insisted. "I must escape from this swamp and you are the only one who can help me. My magic is almost gone."

"I do not believe you," the woman rejoined. "You frighten me. Let me go."

Great Spirit was becoming discouraged but he could not allow the woman's fears to prevail. It was imperative that he win her over.

"I see you have been harvesting medicinal herbs and roots," he said at last. "I also see the harvesting was not good. How many baskets do you have?"

"Only one," she replied, sadly. "I will have to come again tomorrow although I do not like coming to the swamp."

"Look again at your harvest, woman," Great Spirit said. "You will see that your one basket has become five and all are filled to overflowing."

The woman looked and was astounded that what the frog said was true.

"How can this be?" she asked. "It is magic."

"Indeed it is," the frog replied. "I made it so with the last ounce of my power. Unfortunately, now I have no magic left and if you will not help me I will have to do Swamp Spirit's bidding. The results will be tragic for your people and everyone else on earth."

The young woman now knew the frog was a good spirit, for had he been evil he would have destroyed her harvest rather than increase it.

"Come into the canoe," she ordered. "We will have to make great speed if we are to escape the swamp before the sun sets."

However, Swamp Spirit had seen the woman talking to the frog and made ready to prevent her from rescuing him. He took the form of a whirlpool and tried to upset the canoe. But the girl was an expert paddler and easily steered around the menace.

Then Swamp Spirit turned himself into a huge patch of weeds in order to snarl the canoe and prevent its progress. But the girl swung close to the shore and steered among the rocks so that the weeds could not follow. Finally, Swamp Spirit became a heavy wind and caused waves that could upset the canoe. But the girl, who had learned how to handle a canoe from her father and brothers, expertly headed the bow directly into each wave as it appeared and by so doing kept the canoe upright.

Finally the entrance to the swamp was upon them and the canoe glided into the peaceful waters of the lake. The second the swamp was behind them, Great Spirit's powers returned to him. He turned and with a mighty breath blew a storm against the swamp. Swamp Spirit was bowled over by the gust and tumbled backward into some rapids which spun him about so much that by the time he could break loose he was dizzy and exhausted.

The woman, who now knew her passenger was indeed a powerful and good spirit, paddled to her village. There she was greeted by her father and brothers who listened patiently to her story. They all thought she had been overcome by noxious fumes that lurk in swamps. However, they knew better than to laugh at her. She would, they muttered to each other, feel better after a bowl of herbal tea and a night of good rest.

It was not until she picked up the frog and carried it to her lodge did they realize that this was indeed no ordinary frog. They all knew she was terrified of frogs. Her father and brothers picked up the baskets of herbs and followed her to the lodge.

Once inside, Great Spirit made himself known to the chief, the chief's sons and his rescuer. He told them of his adventure in the swamp and sang a song of praise to the brave woman who had agreed to rescue him. Then he made to the chief's entire tribe a great award.

"From this time onward your people will be known as the Frog People. Your totem will be a frog and through it I will protect you for all time."

The following morning Kwa'te departed for his home on the moon. True to his word the Frog People became prosperous and were protected by Great Spirit.

Kwa'te, however, was unable to forget the young woman who had rescued him from the clutches of Swamp Spirit. He finally realized that she meant a great deal to him. He gathered his traveling gear once again and returned to earth. Without delay he went directly to the village of the Frog Princess. He was recognized and made welcome by the Frog Chief. He was taken directly to the great lodge. Kwa'te asked to see the princess and she was ushered into his presence. He greeted her warmly and gave her a present of a pretty necklace carved from fine jade. Then he held out his hand to the young woman. She uncertainly, for she knew not what he intended, took his hand.

"It is fitting," Kwa'te said to the Chief of the Frog People, "that the Great Spirit should have a wife. I would request of you that you give me your daughter to be my wife. She will live with me in my lodge on the moon. She will never grow old but will live forever."

So it was that the daughter of the chief of the Frog People became Great Spirit's wife. The ceremony joining the two in marriage was duly held and the people rejoiced.

After several days of dancing and feasting it was time for the two to depart for Great Spirit's lodge on the moon. The young woman said good-bye to her father, gathered her belongings and placed them in a sack, which she strapped to her back. Then the Great Spirit and his bride took the shapes of hummingbirds and flew away. They have been happy together ever since.

Although the Frog Princess never returned to earth, Great Spirit made it possible that the people could see her once each month—on occasion twice a month. To this day, if you look at the moon when it is full you will see two figures. The larger one is that of Great Spirit. Directly behind him, her bundle of belongings still on her back, is the Frog Princess. Together they look down from the moon's surface and will do so forever.

A Legend of Lake Kalamalka

(An Okanagan Legend)

Lake Kalamalka lies a short distance south of Vernon, B.C., which is a city at the northern end of the Okanagan Valley. The word Kalamalka is from a dialect of an Okanagan Valley tribe of the Shuswap Nation.

For many generations travelers have been awed by the beauty of this unusual body of water. On sunny days the water presents varied hues of brilliant colors. Some days it is a solid color but on others it shows all the colors of the rainbow in rapid changes.

Many of those who have seen this lake claim the colors are caused by the sunlight as it reacts to metallic elements on the lake's bottom. They believe the sand and rocks at the bottom are so filled with metallic ore that they glint and reflect the sun's light back to the surface whereupon the colors appear on the water. However, scientific minds are not always correct.

There is another, entirely different interpretation of the cause of Kalamalka's coloring and many of those who have seen the lake agree with them and reject the scientific explanation.

Many centuries ago long before Tyee Sahale, the Great Spirit, placed humans on his world, giants roamed the land. These giants had been put on earth by Tyee Sahale to do certain works for him. They dug riverbeds, scooped out basins for lakes and caused the great valleys to be dug. After they had completed their work and all the rivers and lakes had been filled and all the valleys had been formed, Tyee Sahale allowed them to stay on the land so they could enjoy the products of their labors.

The giants became hunters and fishermen and did everything present-day humans do. So long as they obeyed his laws, Great Spirit told them, they would be allowed to stay. For many centuries they obeyed the laws of Tyee Sahale and lived peaceful lives.

Then one day, following a great rain storm, there appeared in the sky a huge, beautiful rainbow that stretched across the entire land from the east mountains to the ocean. It was so beautiful the giants knew it had been placed there by Tyee Sahale. But they did not know the reason.

After a few days had passed, the giants decided it had been placed for their use and began to consider ways of dividing the many colors among them. They wanted the colors so they could dye their clothing and ceremonial robes in bright shades.

The Thunderbird, who is Tyee Sahale's greatest spirit, heard them talking and came to the giants. He warned them not to touch the rainbow because Tyee Sahale had placed it in the sky so that he could admire it himself. But the giants would not listen and continued with their plans to take the rainbow for their own uses.

The leader of the giants, however, wanted the rainbow for himself. He looked at it for a long time and decided it would make a perfect bow for his own use. With such a great weapon, he reasoned, he could become the mightiest hunter in the entire world. He made plans to capture the rainbow for himself.

Early the very next morning, before the other giants were ready to venture forth to take the rainbow from the sky, he left his lodge and strode across the valley to where one end of the rainbow was located. He climbed a high mountain, reached up and grasped the rainbow in his mighty fist, wrenched it from the sky and carried it to the ground. There he stood it on end, secured a bow string on it and turned it on its other end where he tied the other end of the bowstring. It was a beautiful bow, so nicely curved.

The giant tested his new bow; he drew back the bowstring and the great bow bent in a perfect arc. He was pleased with his new weapon.

Tyee Sahale, however, had been watching and grew greatly disturbed.

He cast a magic spell and the rainbow shattered into thousands of tiny pieces that fell to the ground.

The leader of the giants was greatly saddened by his loss but did not feel sorry for what he had done. He returned to the village and told his people the great rainbow had fallen down and broken. He told them they could have it to use as dye for their clothing and ceremonial robes. The people rushed to gather the pieces.

But Tyee Sahale summoned the spirit of the east wind.

"Go to where my beautiful rainbow lies in pieces," Great Spirit told East Wind. "Make a mighty blow and push the pieces into the lake that lies nearby. I will decide what to do with it later."

East Wind did as he was told. He blew the pieces into the nearby lake just as the giants rushed up to gather them for their own use. The giants stood on the shore and watched the pieces sink beneath the surface.

Great Spirit was mightily displeased with the giants and sent the Thunderbird to them. Thunderbird told them they had disobeyed the laws of Tyee Sahale and they would be punished. He then cast a spell on the giants and one by one they were turned into the great trees we now call Sitka spruce.

Then Tyee Sahale gathered the pieces of his beautiful rainbow from the lake and fashioned them into a great many small rainbows. This time, though, he made them so they would only last a short while. He did not want anyone ever again to try to capture a rainbow for his own use. That is why you can never find the ends of a rainbow.

These new, smaller rainbows he gave to the gentle rain spirit, the daughter of South Wind. He told her she should place one rainbow into the sky after each shower she would send to the land. The gentle spirit took all the rainbows and saw there were enough to last for all time.

But Tyee Sahale had not gathered all the pieces from the lake. He had left a great number remaining on the sandy bottom. He did this so people would be reminded of the origins of rainbows for all time. He cast a magic spell on the pieces so that when they see the sun they begin to glow and their light rises to the surface of the lake. There they turn the water into many colors.

When the first humans came to the earth and saw the lake of many colors they knew it was a gift from Tyee Sahale and made it into one of their favorite places. They called the lake Kalamalka because that word means "many colors."

The Legend of the Salmon People

(A Tsimshian Legend)

The Salmon People lived on the far side of the wide ocean. Because they were from different families that had different traits, they lived in five separate villages. Because the Great Spirit had so ordained it, these people were much like humans are now. They lived on the land and did many things such as build lodges and carve totems. Each year the oldest from each of the Salmon People's five villages changed into their fish forms. They then began a long journey as they swam from their side of the ocean to the Skeena River. There they swam upstream against the swift flow of the river into small creeks where they would lay eggs. Then, exhausted from the journey, they would die.

The eggs they laid would hatch in early spring and the tiny salmon would leave the Skeena to begin their long swim across the ocean to the villages of their families. Then they would change to human form to await their own final journey back to the Skeena.

The five villages on the far side of the ocean were each some distance from its closest neighbor. Those who lived in the farthest village always set out first, and as they passed the others they called out that the time had come to begin the journey. When the call was heard as the first villagers passed, the Salmon People in the second village began preparing for the journey. Thus, those of the second village arrived several weeks after those of the first and so on until the coho village was passed. Because the Coho People lived in the nearest village they were always the last to leave.

This plan had been worked out by Ka'ah the Great Raven during the very early days of the world and it worked very well indeed. By having the five different families arrive at the mouth of the Skeena at different times, there was always lots of room for everyone. It also meant fishing was good throughout the entire year.

That is the reason there are five species of salmon and why each species arrives during their own predestined time each year.

The Legend of Ghost Lake

(A Shuswap and Carrier Legend)

Not far from the British Columbia town of Quesnel and south of Barkerville, nestled in the forest of tall firs, is a lake known as Ghost Lake. Because it was called Ghost Lake for many years before the arrival of the white man by both the Shuswap people and the Carrier people, that was the name given to it by those who made the first maps of the region.

In the very early years the lake had no name, for it was not the practice of the Indians in that area to name every lake. But, it was well known by the tribes as a lake that was rich in fish and had cold, clear water which was refreshing not only to drink but to swim in as well.

One fine summer day a Shuswap woman and her daughter were picking blueberries along the banks of the lake. They had nearly filled their reed baskets with the delicious berries and were thinking of returning to the village when, suddenly, they were confronted by an evil spirit who had taken over the lake. He turned himself into a large grizzly bear and waded ashore.

"Why are you picking my berries?" the evil spirit asked.

"Forgive us, oh spirit," the frightened woman replied. "We did not know you were master of the lake."

"Now you know," the evil one said. Without another word he struck both the women with his huge claws killing them both. Then he waded back into the lake.

When the women did not return to the village, a search party was sent to look for them. The searchers found their bodies on the lakeshore and carried them home amid wails of sorrow. Their family vowed to avenge their deaths because they could see that a bear had killed them.

The following morning the village chief sent out two of his best hunters to track down the bear and kill it. After two days he sent out another party in search of the hunters. The searchers found the two hunters in the exact spot the women had been found. The hunters were also dead.

Now the villagers realized that it was not a bear who had killed their people and after much discussion decided it was an evil spirit disguised as a grizzly bear. The Shuswap elders decreed that henceforth no one should go near the lake again.

This taboo remained in force for many years and there were no more mysterious deaths. Then, after many years, the Carrier people moved into the area. The two tribes lived in harmony and the Shuswap told the Carrier hunters of the dangers of the lake.

The Carriers, however, chose to ignore the warnings and began to hunt near the lake. One day two hunters failed to return when expected. A search was made and the two hunters were found dead in the exact place the Shuswap had warned the Carrier people to avoid. The elders of the carrier people then decreed the lake to be taboo and it has remained so ever since.

For many years the lake remained quiet and empty. The evil spirit kept to himself but to discourage the people from ever returning he allowed grizzly bears to frequent the region. The bears, thankful for a lake which afforded good fishing, served as his guards. There were so many bears in the woods surrounding the lake that no one, not even the white trappers who came later, would venture along its shores.

Even today the Shuswap, Carrier and white people who inhabit the region, though they now have doubts that the evil spirit owns the lake, avoid venturing along the shore because the bears, as if they are still guarding to the evil one, are so numerous they make it extremely danger-ous for anyone who might foolishly come too close to Ghost Lake.

The Legend of the Magic Halibut

(A Bella Coola Legend)

Long ago the Queen Charlotte Islands were all together as one large island. One morning a fisherman ventured out in his boat to try his luck. He fished all day without catching anything and finally decided to go back to the village.

As he was pulling in his net, a small halibut became tangled in the cords. The fisherman was disappointed with the size but kept it because at least he could say he had not been totally devoid of luck.

His wife, though, was not amused. She was so disgusted at the small fish she tossed it disdainfully on the beach and stalked off in anger.

The halibut, however, was a magic fish and began thrashing around in anger at being tossed aside with so little regard. As he grew angrier, he became larger until finally he was so big his thrashings began to break up the land.

Finally, its enormous size proved too much for the island and it split in two pieces. The halibut kept thrashing around until he had smashed even more of the land. These smaller pieces became islands on their own.

The violence of the magic halibut frightened the people. Many hid in their lodges but others fled to the smaller islands. Once there, they decided to stay.

In the meantime the magic halibut thrashed his way back into the ocean and disappeared.

That is why the Queen Charlotte Islands are the way they are today.

The Journey of Greatest Coyote and Eagle

(As related by a Yakima shaman to the author)

Greatest Coyote was the most intelligent of the animals. He was cunning and possessed powerful magic. Great Spirit had given him special powers so that he might lead the other animals and keep them safe from evil spirits. Greatest Coyote used his powers in the wisest of ways for many years. His magic far surpassed that of any of the other Supernatural Animals. Because he had such great magic, others sought him out when they needed a special favor. For that reason Kwi-Kwi, the eagle, visited Coyote's lodge one day.

Coyote was pleased to see Kwi-Kwi. The two were dear friends but had not seen each other for some time. This was because Kwi-Kwi had become a recluse when his wife died. The couple had been together for many years, had raised many eaglets and lived only to serve each other. When his wife died and passed over to the Land of Mists, Kwi-Kwi in his intense loneliness had retired to his lodge high in a forest tree and was not seen again for a long time.

Finally, however, his grief had driven him to the point where he felt he could no longer live without his beloved wife. He sang songs of praise to the Great Spirit in an effort to convince the Great Spirit to return his wife to him. Great Spirit replied that such a thing could not be done although he offered to find Kwi-Kwi a new mate. This Kwi-Kwi did not want, so he decided to ask Coyote if he could help in some way.

When Kwi-Kwi told his story and explained his loneliness Greatest Coyote listened sadly. He explained to Eagle that entry into the Land of Mists was restricted to those who had been called by the Great Spirit, a call which came only at the end of life. He tried to tell him that intrusion to the Land of Mists was possible only if the intruders had the power to remain invisible so the Keepers could not see them.

Eagle, of course, knew about the Keepers and how they were empowered by Great Spirit to detain the souls of the dead. But his love for his wife was far stronger than his fear of the Keepers.

"You possess the magic," Eagle reminded Coyote, "that can make me invisible so I can elude the Keepers and rescue my wife."

"Yes, I have such magic," Coyote replied, "but I would have to accompany you every step of the way. Besides, my magic has certain limits and I am not sure I want to risk the wrath of the Keepers should my magic fail."

He knew it would be futile to simply tell Eagle that what he asked was not possible. This was something Eagle would have to find out the hard way so Coyote decided to help him. He told Eagle to return to his lodge and gather enough food to last for five days then on the following morning to meet him on the shore of the lake that lay nearby. Kwi-Kwi flew off to gather the supplies he would need.

The following morning the two friends met as planned. Coyote had his canoe ready and the two pushed it away from the shore, clambered aboard and soon were paddling toward the Lands of Mists.

After three days and nights of steady paddling the canoe approached the mist-enshrouded coastline of a very large island. They silently swung the bow of the boat toward the shore. Within a few minutes they were within sight of dry land. As they approached the misty shore, the fog became thicker and they could see only a short distance ahead. Kwi-Kwi suggested he fly high above in order to get a better view but Coyote told him he must not leave the canoe.

"I have sprinkled magic dust over the canoe which will keep us from being seen by the Keepers," said Coyote. "If you leave, they will see you and will detain you forever. You know it is forbidden to enter the Land of Mists before you are called."

Kwi-Kwi said nothing more but paddled silently. He was beginning to think the idea of going to the Land of Mists was not such a good idea after all. However, his love for his wife was stronger than his fear.

Coyote, meanwhile, laid his own plans as he paddled. He knew his tactic was dangerous, that it might cost him his powers and cost Eagle his life, but he felt his magic was strong enough to keep the two out of great danger. His immediate concern was to avoid detection by the Keepers.

Just as the canoe touched the shore Coyote sprinkled more magic dust over both Eagle and himself. They hid the canoe in a thick bush and then made their way inland. Coyote hoped his magic was strong enough to keep them invisible until their quest was ended.

After the two had walked inland for a full day, they spied a great lodge in a large clearing. In the clearing were many beings doing many different things. Some were dancing, others were weaving baskets and blankets, others were singing praises to the Great Spirit. Whatever they were doing it was obvious that all were happy in their tasks.

"See, Eagle," Coyote spoke to his friend. "All are happy. This is the final journey of life. It is the reward for a life of worthy deeds. It would be wrong for you to return your wife to the earthly world."

"Perhaps it would," Eagle replied, "but I feel she should be given the chance. Can it do any harm to find her and ask?"

"I know it to be wrong," Coyote replied. "But I will accompany you if you wish to find her and ask her."

The two then moved into the clearing and walked among the spirits. Eagle noticed how happy they all seemed. They all sang as they carried out their various activities. He noticed that none frowned nor showed any signs of sadness. He also noticed how pale they all were. Although they had their earthly shapes, they were more like smoke. All were nearly transparent. He began to feel that Coyote was right. Perhaps it was wrong to expect anyone to return to the world of earthly existence. He was about to tell Coyote that he wished to return to the canoe and leave the Lands of Mists when he saw his wife. His thoughts of departure were quickly forgotten.

Eagle's wife sat alone weaving a blanket of the most splendid hues Eagle had ever seen. His wife appeared even more beautiful than she had in life. Her eyes had a delicate glow and on her face was a smile of peace and contentment. His love for her coursed through his veins. He could barely contain the excitement of seeing her.

"Coyote," he called, "it is her. Have you ever seen her looking so beautiful and radiant?"

"No, Kwi-Kwi," Coyote replied, "I never have." He remembered how pretty she had been in life. Now she was truly luminous.

"I must take her home with me," Eagle said at last. "Will you help?"

Coyote replied that he would but he reminded Eagle that he was making a terrible mistake. He admonished his friend to think the situation over. But, Eagle was adamant. He wanted his wife back.

"Very well, dear friend," Coyote said, after a moment of thought. "It is a grave error on your part but I will not desert you now. However, this is something you must do all by yourself for I cannot help you.

"Gather one of the sacks which lay piled near the lodge. Place the spirit of your wife in it and then run as fast as you can to where the canoe is hidden." He paused to give Eagle a chance to change his mind.

"I will meet you there and we will make our escape. Because I will not be with you, you will no longer be invisible. If the Keepers see you all will be lost."

With that Coyote melted away into the shadows and began his journey back to the canoe. He was disappointed that his original plan was not working. He had hoped Eagle would see how happy his wife was in the afterlife and would decide to leave in peace. Now he was fearful for he knew what would happen when Eagle returned to the earthly world with his wife's spirit. He wished he had never become involved.

Meanwhile, Eagle had removed one of the sacks from the pile, had crept up behind his wife's spirit, and in one quick movement had captured her and stuffed her into the bag. Quickly he ran from the lodge.

Because he was no longer invisible, he kept to the shadows, dodging from tree to tree while keeping in the thick bush as much as possible. By so doing he managed to avoid detection by the Keepers. He arrived at the canoe only a short time after Coyote had got there.

Within seconds the canoe was pushed off and the escape was underway.

"We will be safe once we have paddled half the width of the lake," Coyote informed Eagle. "Once we are at the halfway point, the spirit in the sack will retake its earthly size and weight once more. You must open the sack at that time so she does not turn to dust inside the sack."

"I will do as you say," replied Eagle. "I will be so happy to see my dear wife once again."

"I do not think you will," was all that Coyote said.

After a day and night of paddling, the middle of the lake was reached. As Coyote had warned, the spirit inside the sack began to take on earthly weight and size. Eagle quickly moved to open the sack and release his wife. His face was aglow with a happy light as he pulled open the sack and looked inside. Then he recoiled in horror. He looked at his friend, his face contorted in confusion and terror. Suddenly he knew what Coyote had been trying to tell him all along.

As Coyote had stated, Eagle's wife was in the sack. She was alive, but she was not as she had been in life. The decay of the grave was on her, her burial clothes had rotted away and her body was withered and dried. Her once-beautiful feathers were dull and had curled at the edges. She reached out from the sack searching for Eagle's hand. He shrank from the touch. With eyes wide with horror, unable to speak, he looked to Coyote for guidance.

"It is as I was trying to tell you, my dearest friend," Coyote said gently. "What passes into the Land of Mists is the spirit. The earthly body remains behind to return to the clay from which Great Spirit fashioned it so long ago. Now, perhaps, you can understand why Great Spirit denied your prayers to return your wife to you."

"I understand," Eagle replied. "But what do I do now? I have stolen my wife's spirit from the Lands of Mists. How can I return it?"

"Keep the sack closed while I turn the canoe around. We are but a few yards from the midway point. Once we cross over your wife will return to her spirit form."

"How will we return her spirit, Coyote? By now the Keepers will be alerted to what I did."

"Fear not, Eagle," Coyote replied. "Once the spirit has regained its proper form simply open the sack. The spirit will rise out and make its way to the clearing from whence it came."

As Coyote guided the canoe past the midway point, the body in the sack returned to spirit form. Eagle opened the sack and his wife's beautiful spirit floated gently into the air above the canoe. Then she paused and spoke to Eagle.

"Oh, my beloved husband," she said very softly, "you did what you did because of your great love for me and because your intention was pure you will not be punished. All that is needed is for you to have learned that those who are gone cannot be brought back. I await your own entry into the Land of Mists when we will be reunited in happiness and love. Meanwhile, remember me as I was in life. We will not remain apart for long."

Then the spirit turned toward the island and disappeared into the mist.

The return journey was made in silence. Coyote was pleased that his friend had learned a great lesson and Eagle was thankful that his wife was happy in the Land of Mists and that she was awaiting his eventual arrival.

The Wisdom of Chief Lolo

(A Shuswap story)

There was once a distinguished chief of the Shuswap nation who was greatly revered by his people and highly respected by the white men who were settling the land. His name was Lolo, but he allowed the white men to call him Jean Baptiste, the name French-Canadian missionaries had given him years before. Many people, both Indian and white, called this great chief St. Paul because he taught his people by telling them stories.

One day a young missionary came to his village to preach to the people. At first his services were quite well attended but soon people tired of his hellfire and brimstone messages and began to stay away. The people would no longer go to his church because the missionary shouted at them and told fearsome stories of an evil place called Hell. He told them they would all go there after death if they did not adopt the religion of the white men. But the religion of the Shuswap people had never included such a dreadful place so they refused to listen to him. Finally the missionary found that no one was attending his services and even those who had embraced the new god began to stay away.

Chief Lolo saw what was happening but said nothing. Instead he stayed in his lodge waiting for the missionary to call on him. At last the missionary came to Lolo for advice. He wanted the old chief to order his people to attend the Sunday service.

Lolo refused that request. Instead he told the missionary a story about two Shuswap artisans who got into a great argument one cold winter day about which one was the better artist. Each insisted he was the greatest carver of jade the village had ever known. Eventually the two agreed to a contest suggested by the village shaman.

The shaman told each of them to take a large block of ice and sculpt it into a smooth, attractive globe that could be put to good use.

Each artist obtained a large block of ice from a frozen river then set about the task of turning it into a beautiful useful object. They started their assignment by hacking and chiseling the ice as they would a piece of rough jade. Despite their efforts, neither could smooth the ice and each ended up with a jagged, cold object that had sharp edges and was not smooth nor round nor attractive and certainly not useful.

As the two sat in dejection feeling humiliated, and the ice sat uselessly in the village circle melting into the ground, the shaman approached carrying a large block of ice which he placed on the ground. Then he pushed aside the axes and chisels and replaced them with a large crock of hot water. He then took a soft cloth of deer hide which he dipped into the hot water. He slowly rubbed the ice all over. Then he dipped the cloth again into the hot water and repeated the process. This he did again and again until the ice block had melted into a smooth, round globe. He called the people to see it and all agreed it was attractive and smooth. Then the shaman carried the ice globe to a large vessel of fresh water and lowered the globe into it.

After a short while the shaman invited the people to drink of the water within. All agreed the water was refreshingly cold.

Chief Lolo turned to the young missionary and said: "You came to my village and tried to hew the people to your beliefs the same way the two artists tried to sculpt their blocks of ice. You ended with the same results and for all your hard work you have achieved nothing but jagged, sharp-edged objects which are of little use to your cause.

"Do as the shaman did. Apply warmth and patience to your subject. As did the block of ice, the people will take the desired shape. They will show no rough edges, and they will also become useful."

The young missionary learned from an old Indian two lessons that night—the first was humility; the second was patience.

Author's note: The Lolo Trail that runs through the Bitterroot Mountains in eastern Idaho is named after Chief Lolo.

The Prayer to Tyee Sahale

(In Chinook)

The Indians who lived along the Columbia River developed a language that became known as Chinook. They were great traders who traveled far and wide moving freely from one tribe to another in their commercial endeavors. Because of this, the Chinook language spread throughout the northwest and became the Lingua Franca of the area we now know as British Columbia, the Yukon, Washington and Oregon. Today the language is little known but there are still a small number of remote tribes where it is the language of common use. The following prayer is ancient and was recited long before the European missionaries arrived. Those who read it cannot help but compare it to The Lord's Prayer. However, it may well be a much older prayer. There is no real way of knowing as the West Coast Natives had no written language.

Several Christian missionaries over the years claimed to have translated The Lord's Prayer into Chinook (and other languages) for the benefit of the Natives, but I personally do not think these claims are true. First, very few missionaries made the effort to learn the many variations and dialects of the many Indian languages, insisting instead the Natives learn English or French. Secondly, because they considered the Natives

Sunday's Child

Meet a child who needs a family

Name, age: Ross, 11.

Background: Ross enjoys just about any sport, whether the game is organized or spontaneous. He likes playing outdoors and riding his bike.

In the sixth grade, Ross benefits from additional academic support, especially in math and reading. He is working on problem-solving and developing social skills.

He does best with a structured routine and clear rules, expectations and limits.

Counseling is helping him prepare for adoption. He would like to maintain contact with biological brothers and a paternal grandmother.

Needed: A two-parent or single-dad family where Ross would be the youngest child. He needs lots of parental time and attention. Adoptive parents must be patient as it might take time for Ross to learn to trust them.

Contact: Northwest Adoption Exchange, 206-441-6822 or www.nwae.org.

Sunday 's Child profiles children in the Northwest Adoption Exchange, a Seattle-based nonprofit for children with special needs who are in state foster care in Washington, Oregon, Alaska and Idaho.

e others' kids

n sto-
now
s that
e ad-
have
that
unity,
r peo-

Long
local
riving
e saw
chok-
t row.
drop
ed the
board

and then addressed the battling kids.

Parents of those students later demanded that she resign from the school board, saying she had no right to get on the bus and reprimand their children. Juster was later cleared by a district investigation.

Today, she stands by what she did. She fondly recalls adults of earlier eras who felt a duty to discipline. As a child, she would visit a friend's home, and if she misbehaved, her friend's mom would make her sit in the corner. Today, she says, if she put a neighbor's kid in the corner, "I'm sure he'd

never be allowed back in my house" — or his parents would call their lawyer.

That mind-set must change, says researcher Gurian. His institute advises mothers and fathers to share parenting duties by creating a team of five or 10 friends, colleagues, neighbors or fellow parishioners. These people can mentor, admonish and love your children, and you can do the same for theirs.

Kids seem to yearn for this sort of attention. As 15-year-old Joe Cypert put it at the teen focus group: "It would be cool to live in a neighborhood like that."

to be pagans and their naturist religion intended for the glorification of heathen idols, they insisted the Natives embrace Christianity. There is little evidence that more than a handful of missionaries made worthwhile efforts to understand the songs, stories, prayers and entreaties the Natives made to the Great Spirit.

Prayer to The Great Spirit

(In Chinook)

Tyee Sahale!
Kla'ksta mitlite kopa sahale,
Kloshe kopa nesika tumtum mika n'em.
Kloshe mika Tyee kopa kona'wa tillicum,
Kloshe miks tumtum kopa illahie,
Kah'kwa kopa sahale.
Potlach kona'wa sun nesika mukamuk.
Spose nesika mamook ma'sachie,
Wake m'ika hyas solleks,
Pe spose klaksa ma'sachie kopa nesika.
Nesika wake solleks kopa klaska.
Mahsh siah kopa nesika kona'wa ma'sachie.

Great Chief who lives in the sky!
Who stays in the sky.
Good is in all our hearts towards your name.
Good Great Chief are you to all friends;
Good is your heart to all the earth
As it is to all the sky.
Give to all each day adequate food.
If we do evil
Be not greatly angry;
And if any do evil towards us
We will not be angry towards them.
Send away far from us all evil.

What the missionaries did was translate the prayer from Chinook into English. And still they could not understand its meaning.

How Deer Tricked Cougar

(A Nootka story)

During the very early days of Great Spirit's world, animals had many human attributes. They lived together in villages. They could talk to each other, which let them tell stories; they could sing, too, which allowed them to sing songs of praises to the Great Spirit. They could use their front paws like hands so were also able to do such things as carve totems in order to leave memorials of their lives and their accomplishments. They kept these attributes for many years until one day Great Spirit took them away from all the animals. He left some of the animals, such as Raccoon and Sea Otter, with limited hand use, but that is another story.

One rainy day a cougar was walking quietly through the woods. He stayed in the underbrush just off the trail because he was looking for a deer whom he thought would make a good supper for him. The deer knew the cougar was behind him so he did not slacken his pace at all but kept a good distance ahead. The reason he did not run was because he knew the cougar had not yet seen him and he did not want to make any sudden moves that would betray his presence to his enemy.

Although the deer proceeded as quietly as possible, he could not help but be distracted by the danger the cougar represented. Because he was thinking more about the cougar than the trail ahead, he grew careless. He looked backwards so often he forgot to look ahead to see where he was going.

Suddenly, he found himself at the bottom of a deep hole. He had not seen it until too late and though he tried to stop he slipped on some wet leaves and slid right down the side of the hole to the bottom.

"Now what will I do?" he thought to himself. "The sides of this pit are too steep to climb and the top is too high for me to jump over. What shall I do? I will die in here."

While he was lamenting his plight the cougar arrived, looked down into the pit and saw the deer at the bottom.

"Hulloah, Deer," the cougar growled. "I seem to have you right where I want you."

The deer looked up. Then he laughed. "No you don't, Cougar," he said after a minute. "I cannot get out but you cannot reach me either. I will die in this pit but at least you will not be able to eat me." Then he laughed again.

The cougar did not like being laughed at because, being a member of the cat family, he was used to having things go his way. He was determined the deer would be his supper. But first he had to get him out of the pit. He sat down to think about how he would do that. No matter how many things he thought of, though, he knew none would work. He decided to forget the entire matter and leave.

"Deer," Cougar said after awhile, "I have to admit you are right. I cannot reach you and you cannot get out. You will not become my supper but I feel bad that you will die down there. We will both be the losers."

Deer agreed that Cougar had a valid point. Deer would not be eaten but he would still be just as dead within a day or two. The situation obviously made him the biggest loser. He began to think.

After a few minutes he called up to see if the cougar was still there. Cougar replied that he was but would not stay because he had to go and find another deer for supper.

"Before you leave," called the deer, "would you be so kind to do me a small favor?"

"If I can," replied the cat. "What do you want me to do for you?"

"As I will surely die down here," the deer replied, "I would like to carve a totem as a memorial to myself. I would like it to show my life's story. Perhaps one day my bones will be found and the finder will know that I was a noble creature of the forest who met his death bravely."

Cougar thought for a moment. At last he said, "I will do that small favor for you, Deer. I will toss down a stout branch from a cedar tree. You can while away your final hours by carving your totem. How large a branch do you need?"

"Not a large one, Cougar, for I am a small animal and need only a small totem. A branch the size of a river otter would do very well."

The cougar looked around and soon found a fine cedar branch, which he tossed into the pit.

"Kla'how'ya, tillicum," he called to the deer. (Tillicum means friend in the Chinook language. "Kla'how'ya Tillicum" means both hello and goodbye.)

"I am sorry that you will end in such a manner. I would have much preferred that you would have become my supper."

Then he quietly slunk away into the bush.

The deer reflected that it was nice of the cougar to refer to him as "tillicum" but decided the cougar was just being sarcastic. He chuckled at how he had fooled Cougar into tossing the cedar branch into the pit. He hoped the plan he had in mind would work.

The deer, you see, had no intention of carving himself a memorial totem. Indeed, he had no intention to die quietly. The minute he knew Cougar had departed, he broke off the pointed end of one of his antlers and with it carved a wooden knife from the cedar branch. He made his knife so it had a long, wide blade and a stout handle. When it was finished, he thought he had carved a very nice knife, indeed. He hoped it was strong enough for what he had in mind.

The deer began scraping at the sides of the pit. At first the soil came away only in small amounts, but as he dug deeper it fell more freely. When the dirt was deep enough to reach his knees he stopped digging and freed himself from the dirt. Then he pounded the dirt until it could support his weight. After he was satisfied that he could stand on the dirt, he scraped more dirt into the hole just as he had done before. Again he pounded the dirt down until it formed a flat top. He continued to dig for many hours being careful to keep the dirt as hard as possible so he could stand on the top.

As the dirt increased in volume, the level increased until at last it was almost to the top of the pit. The digging and piling had taken him all night and part of the morning but he was now more than halfway to the top.

The deer knew the opening of the pit was well within his ability to leap out—and that is exactly what he did.

He gracefully leapt from the floor he had made right onto the ground above. Then he ran quickly to his lodge where he told his story to his family and the other deer in the village. His children thought he was very wise and that he possessed great magic to be able think of such an idea. They sang a song of praise to him.

When they had finished the song he thanked them but then he told them that he succeeded mainly because Cougar had been so easily tricked.

"Cougar thought I was going to die in that hole," he told them. "He would never have helped had he thought I had a plan in mind. He did not help me because of his good nature.

"No one needs great wisdom or powerful magic to survive," Deer added. "What is needed is a desire to live and enough intelligence to think of ways to get out of unfortunate situations."

The Vision of Chief Neewk'klah'kanoosh

(This story was related to me in 1963 by Bill Marshal, a member of the Tsimshian nation.)

"Welcome to my spacious lodge," the old trapper said as I approached. He spoke in the flat monotone of the northern Indian. Then he laughed as he extended his hand in friendship. "I always refer to this as palatial even though it has only one room and a dirt floor."

"At least it has a solid roof," I replied, waving a hand casually toward the three feet of sod on the shack.

"It is a good roof. Keeps the warm inside during winter. Keeps the cool inside during summer. But it sometimes keeps in the smoke and that is not so good."

He brewed up a huge pot of spruce tea as he talked. Then he opened a tin of Hudson's Bay biscuits.

"Have many," he grunted. "Spruce tea is good for you but is bitter. Cookies kill the bitter taste."

I was visiting with an old friend, Billy Marshall. He belonged to some tribe of the Tsimshian nation but I don't think he ever mentioned which one. I had known him for many years and although he was sixty-eight, some forty years older than I, he could still outpace me in the woods.

This had been a chance meeting. I had been wandering around the

B.C.-Yukon boundary doing some research for a book I was thinking about writing some day and had run into him in a little village called, if I recall correctly, Smith River. It was nothing more than a general store and cluster of huts off a narrow dirt road extending north from the Alaska Highway. Billy had been standing outside the store when I wandered into the clearing.

Billy recognized me before I saw him. We had met some years before in Whitehorse. I had flown into the Royal Canadian Air Force base there with an Air Transport Command North Star with a load of material for the base. He had been working on the base as a laborer and had been assigned to help with the unloading. He and I got to talking and I had mentioned my great interest in Indian history. He said he knew a few family legends that he would tell me. From that moment on he and I hit it off very well.

On this particular day, about five years later, we met again. He invited me to his shack for "tea and a biscuit" and I gratefully accepted. Billy, once he got going, was an interesting man to talk with.

So we sat at the rough wooden table, which he had hammered together from some pine planks, talked and whiled away the time. I soon discovered why the spruce tea was less bitter than usual. Billy had liberally laced it with rye whisky.

"What brought you to this neck of the woods?" I asked. "I figured you were set okay up in Whitehorse."

"Nah! Got too crowded. Anyway I wanted to get back to trapping. Besides some damned missionary there was always naggin' at me to go to his church." He paused for a moment as if reflecting. "I hate those guys," he finally continued. "They ruined my people you know."

So we talked about missionaries for a while. I had to agree I thought that overall they had done more harm than good.

"Yeah," Billy retorted. "They came to do good and instead they did well."

Billy! Always the philosopher.

"I see signs that maybe an old prophecy might be comin' true," Billy said at length. "And not afore time either."

"What prophecy?" I asked, my curiosity piqued. Indians have always been great with prophecies, few of which ever come about.

"This one is more of a legend. You still interested in old Indian legends?" he asked.

"Sure am," I replied. "I must have a hundred filed away. I hope to write a book on them one day."

"Good. I got a real interesting one for you. My dad told me it when I was a kid. I've always remembered it. Prob'ly the only thing he ever told me that I remembered."

"All youngsters are the same," I agreed.

"It's a long one," Billy said, "so I better fill up the mugs before I start."

When he sat down again, he stared out the window for a few minutes gathering his thoughts. I stared quietly into my mug of whisky-spruce tea. I had learned long before that it is not wise to interrupt an Indian story-teller while he is thinking. Finally he began.

The Legend

In the last days of the 1850s there lived a Tsimshian chief who was also a shaman. He was named Neewk'klah'kanoosh (pronounced Nu-klaw-kawn-ush). He guided his people well and under his leadership they prospered. Neewk'klah'kanoosh served as chief for many years and was a fairly old man when the first missionaries arrived. Some of the people called them black robes.

While Neewk'klah'kanoosh did not greet the black robes with open arms, he made no effort to hinder their travels among his people. Nonetheless, he was uneasy with their methods and made efforts to temper their zeal to turn the people into white men. One or two listened to him but most did not. The chief tried to explain that Indians were not white, did not understand the ways of the whites and would be better off under their old laws and customs.

The missionaries would not hear of such things. They did everything they could to undo the traditions of centuries—and in most cases were successful. Slowly the Indians surrendered to their demands—even when the missionaries told the children they must no longer talk in any language but English. Later they took the children away to attend white schools.

Neewk'klah'kanoosh watched and was saddened by what he saw happening but could do nothing about the situation except worry. He feared the missionaries would totally destroy the culture in which his people had flourished. He grew particularly alarmed when the missionaries began demanding that lodge poles and totem items be discarded. These things were pagan idols they said and must be destroyed. The old chief was powerless to change things and this saddened him.

One morning he came out from his lodge. He called for his people to gather so he could speak to them. The missionaries heard of the meeting and came to listen but Neewk'klah'kanoosh chased them away. Then, so they could not know what he was going to say, he spoke in the Tsimshian language. This foiled the missionaries as none had bothered to learn the difficult language.

Neewk'klah'kanoosh told his people of a dream he had during the night. The words he used were more or less as follows:

"Last night in a vision I witnessed a great meeting held in a clearing near the edge of a lake. In the clearing I saw the Great Spirit, the Thunderbird, Ka'ah the Raven, the four great winds, the Hummingbird, the spirit of the Moon and the spirit of the Sun. They sat in a half-circle around Great Spirit. All sat very still and in silence while Great Spirit spoke. And the words he spoke caused distress among the lesser spirits.

"'I have looked down on my world with great alarm for I see my children at the brink of a great disaster,' spoke Great Spirit. 'There have come among them a group of white men dressed in black robes each carrying a thick book. These men are luring my children away from the customs and traditions of their fathers and of their grandfathers before them. These men in the black robes tell my children stories of a mighty god whose magic lies within the book they carry. They say my children must follow this new god for his magic is greater than that of the Great Spirit.

"'They are wrong. The god of the black robes is not all-powerful. Their god does not exist outside of their own minds. His magic is without potency. Their god does not come forth to aid the world or to stop drought or to hold back floods. He cannot because his power is no more than the words of the black robes who spread their stories.

"'Still, it must be the people who decide. If they wish to hear the words of the white men, they shall be free to do so. If they choose to follow the ways of their fathers, they shall be free to do that also. I have decided, therefore, to step aside for a time. I will no longer intercede for my children. I will allow them to listen to the white men, to hear their message, to live according to the rules they say are within the book they carry. I will not walk among them again until my children ask me to return.'

"Great Spirit then stopped speaking. Thunderbird asked of him, 'How long will be this time of which you speak?'

"Great Spirit then spoke again. 'The time of which I speak shall be the time it takes for the people to decide the way they shall go. It may be many years or may be but a few. It is up to them.'

"Then Thunderbird spoke. 'If you leave, the evil spirits will grow bold. They will roam the lands. They will cause much trouble to the people. We will be unable to stop them without your great magic.'

"'That is true,' Great Spirit replied. 'The evil spirits will go unchecked. They will cause floods and famines. They will cause wars. They will cause drought. They will rob the people of their senses. My children shall suffer greatly.'

"Hummingbird then spoke. 'Are we not to intervene? Surely, the people will need guidance.'

"Great Spirit replied to Hummingbird, 'Their guidance must come from the men in black robes. They will call upon their god to make things right. They will tell the people to pray and trust in the new god. Nothing will happen. The evil spirits will not stop their mischief. The new god will not keep the evil ones in check because he exists only in the minds of the men in black robes. The people will see this and doubts will arise. Until then, though, my children must decide for themselves.'

"Then Ka'ah the Raven spoke. 'If you are to go for a time then shall we also leave?'

"'No, Ka'ah. You, Thunderbird, Hummingbird, the spirits of the moon and the sun and the four winds shall remain. I am not deserting my children. I am only giving them time to consider.

"'Raven, you shall remain to serve the people as a reminder to them that all things came from the Great Spirit. You, Thunderbird, shall continue to guard my lands. You shall continue to make lightning and to cause the thunder. When they hear and see it the people will remember the magic that once protected them.

"'You, North Wind, will continue to bring the winter cold and the snow. Your two children shall control the ice and the snow. South Wind, you will bring the Spring. Your children will bring the warm winds, the gentle rains and the cooling breezes.

"'East and West Winds, you will bring the breezes that will dictate the rage or tranquility of the seas. Your children will make the mist, the gentle zephyrs and the cooling breezes to the flowers of the meadows. These things will remind the people that the magic of Great Spirit remains.'

"Then Hummingbird spoke. 'What, oh Great Spirit, will I do?'

"Great Spirit spoke again. 'You, Hummingbird, will continue your flights across the evening and the morning skies. You will control the day's weather as you have for countless centuries. You will remain the beacon to the Winds. When they see the red sky in the morning they will blow storms; but if they see red at night they will bring gentle breezes. These things will be reminders to the people that I have not deserted them.'"

"And then," Chief Neewk'klah'kanoosh continued, "the Moon Spirit spoke. 'How shall I serve you, Great Spirit?' he asked.

"'You, Moon Spirit,' replied Great Spirit, 'will continue to control the tides so the oceans will rise and fall as they have for centuries. You will circle the world each night and will bring some light to the darkness.'

"Then the Sun Spirit spoke. 'And what will I do, oh Great Spirit?'

"Great Spirit answered him in turn. 'You will make your daily journeys as you have for untold centuries. You will heat the land and bring warmth to my children and to my animals and you will warm the mountain lakes and melt the snow on the high peaks in late spring so the streams and rivers may be renewed. You will cast your light upon the earth and make the plants grow. Sometimes I will tell you to bring great heat to my children. That will remind them of the power of my magic.'"

Then Neewk'klah'kanoosh, the great chief, stood and motioned his people to come closer.

"When Great Spirit had spoken to his lesser spirits, he signaled that he would soon depart. But first he spoke these words: 'My people will suffer at the hands of the white men in black robes. Their children shall be wrenched from their mothers' bosoms and sent to villages far away. There they will be forced to live as white children. The men in black robes will be joined by women in black robes. Then shall the children be beaten and mistreated in many other ways. The men in black robes will destroy the totems. They will forbid the people to speak the language of their ancestors. They will bring upon my children terrible diseases and will harm them in a hundred ways. I know this will happen. I have seen it come about in every place the men in black robes have gone before.'

"Great Spirit paused again," said Neewk'klah'kanoosh. "Then he continued. 'The men in black robes have been to many other lands. They have done only mischief everywhere they appeared. There have been wars, floods, disease, hunger and countless calamities. The men in black robes have always promised that their god will set things right but he has never shown himself. That is because he exists only in the minds of the men in the black robes. These things will continue to happen but now my people will be also affected.'"

"Then Raven spoke again," said Neewk'klah'kanoosh. "Raven asked if the men in black robes would endure forever."

"'No, Raven, they will not,' Great Spirit replied. 'Already they fight among themselves. They have divided into many groups and there is no peace among them. Each group sees their god in a different light. Still their god does not appear. That is because he exists only in their minds. My children will see this in time. That is why you must remain. One day they will call for you again.'"

"Thunderbird spoke again," Neewk'klah'kanoosh told his people. "He asked Great Spirit if there would be signs."

"'There will be signs,' Great Spirit told him. 'The signs will be a reawakening among my children. They will once again take up the tools of their fathers' crafts. They will once more carve the red cedar wood, the jade and argillite. The will again paint the symbols of their culture. They will again make masks and they will relearn their dances. They will once more carve the totems and the lodge poles. They will have ancestral lands returned to them and they will once again govern themselves. The children will learn the language of their grandparents, the ones their own parents were denied. Then they will cast off the men in black robes and return to their trust in the Great Spirit.'

"And with that Great Spirit rose into the sky and was gone.

"That was my dream," Neewk'klah'kanoosh told the gathered people. "It was a vision. It told me that Great Spirit will return. It told me the world will continue but the next many years will be very hard for our people. It told me that one day Great Spirit will return."

Then the great chief returned to his lodge. The people looked at the men in black robes and wondered about the vision. Just then, though the sky was blue and clear of clouds, there came a mighty thunder clap. The sound resounded through the valley and the people knew that Neewk'klah'kanoosh had seen in his dream a true look at the future. Many wondered when his prophecy would come about. Others wondered if it would. The men in black robes gathered the village children into a circle. The daily lesson about the new god was beginning. They had not heard the words Neewk'klah'kanoosh had spoken. Nor would they have cared, for they did not understand the message.

"Well," said Billy. "What do you think of that?"

I didn't answer right away because I was still busy scribbling the basics of his narration. When I was finished, I put aside my pad and sat silently for some time while Billy refilled my mug with tea.

"I hope," I said finally, "that it will all come true. It would be a good thing. Your people are not white men. They should never have been forced into a life that was so alien to them. I hope Chief Neewk'klah'kanoosh was right."

"Let's drink to Neewk'klah'kanoosh," said Billy.

And we did.

Ah Mo: Indian Legends
Tren Griffen
ISBN 0-88839-244-3
5.5 x 8.5 • sc • 64 pp.

American Indian Pottery
Sharon Wirt
ISBN 0-88839-134-X
5.5 x 8.5 • sc • 32 pp.

Argillite
Drew/Wilson
ISBN 0-88839-037-8
9 x 12 • hc • 313 pp.

Art of the Totem
Marius Barbeau
ISBN 0-88839-168-4
5.5 x 8.5 • sc • 64 pp.

Best of Chief Dan George
Chief Dan George &
Helmut Hirnschall
ISBN 0-88839-544-2
5.5 x 8.5 • sc • 128 pp.

Bird of Paradox
Gene Anderson
ISBN 0-88839-360-1
5.5 x 8.5 • sc • 320 pp.

Buffalo People
Mildred V. Thornton
ISBN 0-88839-479-9
5.5 x 8.5 • sc • 208 pp.

Coast Salish
Reg Ashwell
ISBN 0-88839-009-2
5.5 x 8.5 • sc • 88 pp.

Eskimo Life of Yesterday
Revillion Freres
ISBN 0-919654-73-8
5.5 x 8.5 • sc • 48 pp.

Haida
Leslie Drew
ISBN 0-88839-132-3
5.5 x 8.5 • sc • 112 pp.

Indian Art & Culture
Kew/Goddard
ISBN 0-919654-13-4
8.5 x 11 • sc • 96 pp.

Indian Healing
Wolfgang Jilek
ISBN 0-88839-120-X
5.5 x 8.5 • sc • 184 pp.

Indian Herbs
Ray Stark
ISBN 0-88839-077-7
5.5 x 8.5 • sc • 48 pp.

Indian Hunters
Stephen Irwin
ISBN 0-88839-181-1
5.5 x 8.5 • sc • 296 pp.

Indian Quillworking
Christi Henslen
ISBN 0-88839-214-1
5.5 x 8.5 • sc • 64 pp.

Indian Rock Carvings
of the Pacific Northwest
Beth Hill
ISBN 0-919654-34-7
5.5 x 8.5 • sc • 40 pp.

Indian Tribes
of the Northwest
Reg Ashwell
ISBN 0-919654-53-3
5.5 x 8.5 • sc • 74 pp.

Indians of the
Northwest Coast
David Allen
ISBN 0-919654-82-7
5.5 x 8.5 • sc • 32 pp.

Iroquois:
Their Arts and Crafts
Carnie Lyford
ISBN 0-88839-135-8
5.5 x 8.5 • sc • 96 pp.

Kwakiutl Legends
James Wallas
ISBN 0-88839-230-3
5.5 x 8.5 • sc • 216 pp.

More Ah Mo
Tren Griffen
ISBN 0-88839-303-2
5.5 x 8.5 • sc • 64 pp.

Northest Native Arts:
Basic Forms
Robert E. Stanley Sr.
ISBN 0-88839-506-X
8.5 x 11 • sc • 64 pp.

Northest Native Arts:
Creative Colors 1
Robert E. Stanley Sr.
ISBN 0-88839-532-9
8.5 x 11 • sc • 32 pp.

Northest Native Arts:
Creative Colors 2
Robert E. Stanley Sr.
ISBN 0-88839-533-7
8.5 x 11 • sc • 24 pp.

Potlatch People
Mildred Valley Thornton
ISBN 0-88839-491-8
5.5 x 8.5 • sc • 320 pp.

Spirit of Powwow
Kay Johnston &
Gloria Nahanee
ISBN 0-88839-520-5 sc
ISBN 0-88839-551-5 hc
8.5 x 11 • sc • 144 pp.

Those Born at Koona
C/J Smyly
ISBN 0-88839-101-3
5.5 x 8.5 • sc • 120 pp.

Tlingit Art:
Totem Poles & Art of the
Alaskan Indians
Gloria Williams &
Maria Bolanz
ISBN 0-88839-509-4 sc
ISBN 0-88839-528-0 hc
8.5 x 11 • sc • 208 pp.

Tlingit: Their Art
& Culture
David Hancock
ISBN 0-88839-530-2
5.5 x 8.5 • sc • 96 pp.

Totem Poles of the
Northwest
David Allen
ISBN 0-919654-83-5
5.5 x 8.5 • sc • 32 pp.

When Buffalo Ran
Ruth Johnston
ISBN 0-88839-258-3
5.5 x 8.5 • sc • 128 pp.

hancock
house

View all **HANCOCK HOUSE** *titles at* www.hancockhouse.com